THE WEDDING PARTY

Other books by Elisabeth Rose:

Coming Home
Instant Family
Outback Hero
The Right Chord
Stuck
The Tangled Web

THE WEDDING PARTY

•

Elisabeth Rose

AVALON BOOKS
NEW YORK

Published by Avalon Books,
an imprint of Thomas Bouregy & Co., Inc.
160 Madison Avenue, New York, NY 10016

Library of Congress Cataloging-in-Publication Data

Rose, Elisabeth, 1951-
    The wedding party / Elisabeth Rose.
        p. cm.
    ISBN 978-0-8034-7657-8
    1. Weddings—Fiction.   I. Title.
    PR9619.4.R64W53 2011
    823'.92—dc22

                                2010044008

PRINTED IN THE UNITED STATES OF AMERICA
ON ACID-FREE PAPER
BY RR DONNELLEY, BLOOMSBURG, PENNSYLVANIA

To Colin, Carla, and Nick

Acknowledgments

I would like to thank and acknowledge my niece Cath and her husband Andy, whose wedding gave me the idea for this story and who answered my questions and generously allowed me to use various elements of their big, beautiful day. None of my characters' disasters are based on their wedding, I hasten to add.

Many thanks also to my sister-in-law turned tour guide Judy, who provided information about Narooma. Thanks, Judy and John, for your hospitality on my research trip to the coast.

My dentist unexpectedly provided a key plot point during a routine checkup, proving that writers can pick up useful tips anywhere and everywhere.

Thanks also to my friends Joanne and Caroline, who gave me the specific information about dental work from both sides of the reclining chair.

Chapter One

Brady, eyes red rimmed, leaden, and rasping against the lids, scanned the tiny Moruya airport building for his mates. It didn't take long for him to ascertain they weren't there. The waiting area was the size of a large living room, with about six chairs—two occupied—a deserted car-hire booth on the left, and one man in official gray shirt and shorts lounging behind a small check-in counter on the right. Three of Brady's fellow passengers were greeting friends enthusiastically as they headed for the open door. An athletic-looking elderly couple, who had also been on his flight, had already disappeared.

He lifted his bag, replaced his dark glasses, and stepped into the barrage of sunlight and heat bouncing off concrete and tar. The gray-haired pair finished stuffing themselves into the rear of a cab—the only cab. It took off, leaving Brady standing in the sun, scowling at what resembled a paddock but was really the parking area. The other three arrivals, two young men and a woman, were stowing gear into a large red four-wheel drive, shouting and laughing with their mates.

His body had the strength and vitality of chewed string, a persistent triangle player had taken up residence in his ears, and his sinuses were clogged after hours of breathing recycled air. Plus there was the aching molar that had started up somewhere along the way. A sensitivity to cold food had developed into an annoying, constant background pain. He probed with his tongue. Tender gum.

All his flights had been late except this last one from Sydney to Moruya, and because of the delays, he'd had to scramble for the connection. His brain had been left behind en route, maybe in Singapore. His body? Who knew?

Where was Alex? The least he could do was turn up to collect his best man after a crippling twenty-eight hours of travel. What a nightmare planes were. Give him the sea any day.

He dumped his bag close to the dirty beige-painted wall in the shade of a lone palm tree and folded his arms. Apart from the airport terminal, which was really not much more than a shed, and other hangar-type buildings behind the perimeter fence, there were no permanent structures in sight. Tents from the beachside camping ground he'd seen from the air as they'd come in were just visible behind a row of Norfolk Island pines a few hundred meters beyond the parking lot.

Doors slammed on the four-wheel drive. He had no idea where this house they were all staying in was. Moruya was the closest town. He had to go farther south to Narooma. Should he cadge a lift to Moruya or wait? The decision was suddenly made easy by a lung-collapsing burst of black diesel exhaust as the four-wheel drive blasted off. The girl waved to him as they shot by.

Phone. In his bag. He unlocked it, unzipped it, and felt about in an inner pocket. *Got it.* Rezipped the bag. Yawned a face-cracking yawn, blinked, and stretched his eyes wide to focus, then yawned again, concentrated, and pressed the right buttons. After many rings, Alex answered. He sounded worse than Brady felt. He sounded terminal.

"Brady," he croaked. "You made it. Sorry, mate, I'm half dead with flu. We're still in Canberra." There was a burst of coughing. Brady winced, grimacing, and held the phone away from his ear until the wheezing subsided. "Sorry," Alex said. "Phoebe's collecting you. Isn't she there?"

"No. You sound terrible." Who on earth was Phoebe? Had they met?

"She won't be long. We'll be down as soon as I can travel." There was another burst of coughing, followed by a wheezing groan. Was this the end of Alex? Was his bride fated to be widowed before she was married?

"Brady?" A woman's voice was suddenly in his ear. "Hi, it's Lindy. I'm so glad you made it safely. As you can hear, Alex is really sick, and we're praying to every god known to man he'll be better by the weekend." She laughed, but it crackled and snapped in his ear like breaking ice. She was a girl on the edge.

"He'll be fine. He's tough as old boots."

She surged on. "Phoebe Curtis is picking you up and taking you to the house, so make yourself at home. Dave and Angela are arriving on Thursday, and Sophie and Kate are coming with us—whenever that is." Her voice wavered. "I wanted this to be such a fun week together before the wedding, and now . . ." She sniffed.

Brady grimaced again. What could he say? Before his fuzzy brain could come up with something suitably reassuring, sympathetic, and consoling, Alex's scraping voice came back on the line.

"Lindy's having kittens here. On top of this flu, the caterers want to change the menu"—cough, cough, cough—"from a salmon mousse starter to melon and avocado. Five days before the wedding. It's tough doing everything long-distance."

"I bet," Brady said helplessly. He had no idea what was involved with organizing a wedding. How hard could it be? Wasn't it basically a party? All you needed was someone to tie the knot, booze, friends, and a barbecue. Or maybe he'd been at sea too long.

"Make yourself at home. We'll be there in a day or two. Ciao, mate."

"Right," said Brady to a dead line. Poor Alex. But salmon? Melon? Who cared? And what did Phoebe Curtis look like? More to the point, where was she?

He rubbed his hands over his face and sniffed. The warmth of the morning sun was bringing out the staleness in his clothes, very noticeable in this fresh, clean country air. He needed a shower and coffee. And sleep. With any luck his tooth would settle down when his body was rested. He'd give Phoebe five minutes, then go inside and organize a hired car. Better to be independent, anyway. A means of escape might become a necessity if he was confined in a few days to a house full of women intent on fussing about the wedding. There was nothing worse than a freaked-out bride worrying whether her guests ate salmon or melon. Why didn't they elope and get the technicalities over with, then throw a monster party? Much more fun and stress free for everyone.

Two minutes later a bright yellow VW Beetle screeched to a halt in front of him. A woman in big, round, dark glasses and a white tank top bounced out of the driver's side, stared for a moment with her mouth open, then called over the roof of the car between them, "Are you Brady?"

"Are you Phoebe?"

"Yep. Jump in." She had a smile as bright and sunny as the day. A swath of burgundy-and-copper hair swung as she disappeared into the car. The engine roared. *Must be in a hurry.* He hoisted his bag and opened the passenger door.

"Toss it in the back," she said.

He pulled the seat forward and wrestled his bag into the rear. It was awkward. His knuckles jammed against the doorpost as he tried for the right angle. He swore vile things in Portuguese under his breath.

Phoebe grinned at him from the driver's seat. "Good flight?"

"No." He gave the bag an almighty shove and slammed the front seat into place. It wouldn't click into position properly. More Portuguese.

"You didn't push your bag in far enough. It needs to go further across." She sprang out, leaned into the back, and pulled at his duffel bag. "There."

He slumped into the newly positioned seat and buckled his seat belt. She gunned the engine, and he glanced at her with a frown as it skipped a few beats, then settled into an unhealthy-sounding roar.

Unfortunately, she caught the expression on his face, but it was impossible for him to pretend he was relaxed and happy and excited about a wedding. He was too wrecked to do anything much. Her smile flashed on and off again while she manipulated the gear stick and clutch, which appeared to be as temperamental as the engine. "Beetles are real characters. They all have individual personalities. Have to keep Fred revved up or he stalls."

He gripped the seat as she accelerated around the parking lot, dodging the few parked cars in a wide arc, and careered onto the road to the highway. Fred needed a complete physical and then, probably, euthanasia. "Thanks for picking me up."

"No problem. Alex and Lindy are knee-deep in wedding stuff as it is without him being sick. Rotten timing." She tossed him another cheery grin. "Lindy's super organized, though, so everything will go perfectly, I'm sure. It's so exciting, isn't it?"

He grunted. Tiredness coupled with the freshness of the air and the heat of the afternoon had stupefied his three remaining relatively alert brain cells.

"I love weddings. They're so romantic and everybody's always happy and ready to have a good time."

Another grunt.

"Don't you think so?" She sounded surprised, and when he glanced at her, the smile had faded. He blinked hard, couldn't prevent a yawn but roused himself to be sociable.

"Not particularly. They're all right. So long as they're not mine." He stared out the poky little window. The seat springs had collapsed, so he felt as if he was sitting in a bucket. Beetles weren't designed for tall Aussie men. They were designed for short-legged Germans and their families. His knees were jammed almost under his chin. "How far to the house?"

"It's in Narooma."

That wasn't what he'd asked, but from memory, he knew that the trip was about half an hour. In a bucket. A bucket whose engine sounded sick. After a short tussle with the catch, he opened the quarter pane for a stream of fresh air.

"Where did you guys meet?" she asked.

He took his first good look at her. Her attention was fixed on the highway. Strands of her hair whipped about in the slipstream from the open window. The exposed skin on her arms and throat was honey brown and smooth. She had an attractive little ear on display from this angle, with a gold stud. Her legs, encased in white cargo pants, were slim, ending in painted toenails and sandals. Very nice package indeed. Was she staying in the house too?

"High school. In Melbourne."

"Best friends?"

"Yeah."

"So you've kept in touch. Lots of people don't after they leave school."

"We three did. Alex, Dave, and me," he said. "Sometimes it's years between contact, though."

She nodded. "Lindy's the only school friend I still keep in touch with. It's like that with us too. Could be years between get-togethers, but we pick up where we left off. And I've known Ruth and Phil, her parents, for ages. They were almost a second family for me at one stage."

"Are you a bridesmaid?" Maybe pretty Phoebe would be his partner. Maybe he could entice her to be his partner in more ways than one. They'd be in proximity to each other, sharing a house for the week.

"No. I'm the celebrant."

"The celebrant?" The information bounced off the active brain cells and jerked him upright.

She sent him a half-amused, half-indignant smile. "Why does that surprise you?"

"Every celebrant I've ever seen has been old. Filling in time between retirement and death. Do you live down here?" Along with the retirees and the fringe-dweller hippie types. *Nice place to visit; wouldn't want to live there.*

"For about four years now."

"And is celebrating all you do?"

She laughed. It was a genuinely happy sound. "I wish. Imagine celebrating all your life. No. I work in a secondhand bookshop in Narooma. Weddings are my very favorite thing, though."

"Are you married?"

She shook her head. He leaned back and tried to stretch his legs in the cramped area. She was unmarried and sweet. She talked a lot, but she looked like a girl who'd be up for some fun. Perhaps a little gently amorous playtime, some nibbling of that soft neck and running his hands over those curves . . . His eyes closed. But . . . a celebrant. She spent her life marrying people to each other. No danger of messy aftermath, though. He was only here for a week. . . .

Phoebe glanced at her passenger once or twice and decided, based on the heavy breathing, that he had gone to sleep. Thank goodness for that! He was jet-lagged, poor bloke. She opened her eyes wide and grimaced, releasing a lungful of air. Now she had time to regroup and cobble together her composure, completely mutilated by the sight of Brady Winters.

No one had told her. No one had mentioned how shatteringly sexy he was. Alex might at least have said something to the effect that his best man was a girl's dream come true. Or Lindy might have. Granted, she hadn't met him, but she must have seen photos. How could she not have said anything at all? She could have said, for example, "Pick up Brady at the airport, Pheeb. You can't miss him; he's the sex bomb, the Greek god, the Adonis." Then Phoebe would have been a tiny bit prepared to have her breath whisked from her, and been able to have her brain partially connected to her tongue.

As it was, he'd think she was a babbling, chattering airhead. In fact, he had been rather tight-lipped and unresponsive. But she wouldn't hold curtness against him or blame herself. She would put it down to a murderous flight. When he'd had a sleep and was re-united with his mates, he'd cheer up. And he was there to celebrate his best friend's wedding. He had to be looking forward to that, despite his less-than-enthusiastic response to her comment about weddings.

Her fingers danced a little jig on the steering wheel. This week was going to be such fun when they all arrived. Lindy hoped Alex would be fit enough to travel on Wednesday, so that left the rest of today and tomorrow to fill in with Brady. She could pump him for juicy info on the groom to use in the service and surprise the couple— if she could keep her hands off him. Fancy being alone in a house for two days and nights with a man who was your ultimate fantasy come to life.

She giggled softly and glanced at him again. His head rested on the door frame. Dark glasses hid his eyes, but the stubble on his firm, tanned chin and cheeks gave him a tough, outdoorsy look, which wasn't surprising considering his job crewing on an oceangoing yacht. Rangy, wiry, and fit, he was no fashion slave—that was for sure—dressed for comfort in worn blue jeans, loafers without socks, and a Rolling Stones T-shirt. Part of a tattoo peeked out from under one sleeve. She couldn't see properly what it was. Probably an anchor, like Popeye's.

According to the information Lindy *had* supplied about him, Brady spent his life floating about the oceans of the world as crew member on a millionaire's private yacht. All right when you were twenty, or even thirty, but as Lindy pointedly remarked, "What about when he's fifty? He has nothing. No home, no possessions, no security, no anything." He and Alex and Dave, the other best man, the third member of the trio of best mates, were all thirty-five. Two had settled down. One hadn't and, by the sound of things, wasn't keen to.

So, sexy he might be, but dream come true, not quite. She'd keep that thought in mind when he woke up and during the ensuing days when they were alone together and she was tempted to indulge further in a deadly sin. Apart from anything else, it wasn't a good look for the celebrant to flirt with the best man—or allow the reverse to occur.

Brady woke when the Beetle jerked to a halt. He yawned and rubbed his face. Bristles pricked his fingers. He needed a shave.

"We're here."

He turned in surprise toward the female voice. *Who . . . ? Where . . . ?* Happily smiling Phoebe was next to him. "Sorry. I was asleep. . . ."

"That's okay. You'll need a few days to recover, but it's a great place to do it in. Look."

He did as he was told and saw a timber-framed house nestled among tall spotted gum trees and a lush, flower-filled garden. The land sloped gently away to the water—a bay, not the open ocean, but still beautiful, sparkling blue in the sunlight. The silvery notes of bellbirds chimed from somewhere in the treetops. A wave of familiarity swept over him at the sound. The smell of eucalyptus and the rustle of dry leaves in the hot air reminded him of all those long summer holidays when he'd been a kid—one when he'd vacationed at the coast with a foster family, when he'd fallen in love with the ocean.

"Whose place is it?"

Phoebe opened her door. "Friends of Phil and Ruth. They're away overseas, and they said Lindy could use it. It's really big. Split-level." She got out, leaned over into the back and began tugging at his bag.

"Generous of them. Hey, I'll do that." He flung his own door open.

"I've got it."

The duffel bag fell onto the gravel driveway with a thud before he could extricate himself from his seat belt and untangle his legs. She lifted it with both hands and started for the house. Brady slammed the door, darted forward, and grabbed the strap from her grasp. "Give me that."

She relinquished it with a smile. He followed her jauntily swinging hips up three steps to a wide wooden verandah, which disappeared around both sides of the house. "I'll show you to your room. Girls are on this level; boys are downstairs. There are two bedrooms, a bathroom, and a rumpus room down there. Lindy worked out all the sleeping arrangements and e-mailed me a list and a house plan. She's very organized." The doubtful way she said it implied that she thought a map of the house a bit excessive. He thought it sounded like a woman bordering on insanity.

Whoever those generous owners were, they had taste and style. The house was beautifully furnished, with functional dark wood furniture, a minimum of fussy knickknacks, some very nice landscapes hanging on the clean white-painted walls, and fantastic views of the bay and thick tree-clad slopes on the far shore through wide floor-to-ceiling living room windows.

Phoebe led him down a staircase to the lower level. The rumpus room stretched the width of the house. At one end was a wet area with a bar and kitchenette; in the center were a pool table, a dining table, and four chairs; and at the far end were a TV and two sofas.

His room faced east, toward the open ocean, although the water wasn't visible. He had a view of heavy-duty natural bushland instead. A bird feeder hung from the roof outside the sliding glass door to a small paved area. Two single beds purred, "Come to me."

"The bathroom's across the hallway," said Phoebe. "Do you need a towel?"

Brady dropped his bag onto the floor. "Umm."

"A towel? Do you have a towel?"

"Yes."

"Would you like to take a shower first and then have something to eat, or the other way round?" She looked at him expectantly. "I can easily whip up a meal, or a snack, if you'd prefer, if you've already eaten—"

He cut into the babble. Too many questions, too many decisions. "Shower, then coffee."

"Right. Fine. Okay." She backed out and closed the door.

"Thanks," he called, but she'd gone—with a look on her face as if he'd slapped her. He hadn't meant to be rude. Had he been? He rummaged for clothes and the towel. Women could be ultrasensitive to some things and not others. Women like Maureen, for example: quick to take offense at the slightest hint of criticism, but very free with her own complaints about his behavior and attitude. Not to mention his absences at sea.

He straightened with a handful of rumpled but clean clothes. A complicated lot, females. He sighed. If only they weren't so darned addictive . . . So much for the Brotherhood. He was the last man standing of that trio of mates whose motto was "Live free; stay free; don't let the turkeys get you down."

They'd all left Australia together after finishing university, intent on exploring the world, leaving their marks, but first Dave, then Alex had succumbed to the lure of a steady income and two feet on a career ladder. Office workers, both of them. Goodness knew what they did all day. Sat on their bums staring at a computer screen.

Sad what falling for a woman could do. Tragic, actually. Alex had always wanted to ride a motorbike from Europe to Asia following the Silk Route, then do the length of the two Americas, north to south. Fat chance now. No matter how wonderful Lindy was, by the sound of her, she wouldn't agree to that. Not if, as Alex had told him, they were buying a house. And Dave and Angela were expecting their first child. Trapped. Ensnared and finished. Not for him. No way, José. He shuddered and went across the hallway to the bathroom.

Brady stood under the shower with his eyes closed, reveling in the luxury of a spacious bathroom and plentiful hot water. His body gradually revived, and stiff muscles loosened. *Marvelous.* Best shower he'd had in ages. He reached for one of three bottles of shampoo lined up in the shower rack, picked the least flowery smelling of them to use in his hair.

Phoebe pounded on the bathroom door. "What?" he yelled.

The door opened a crack. "Brady?"

Good heavens! Was she coming in? Couldn't she wait till he'd finished? "Yes?" he spluttered.

"I'm sorry. I forgot to tell you . . . this area's on water restrictions, and we have to limit our usage. Can you finish up soon, please?"

Blimey! "Sure. Sorry. Didn't realize."

"Thanks." The door closed.

He stuck his head under the spray to rinse away the shampoo and turned off the taps. Phoebe sounded like the headmistress of a boarding school. Was she staying here even though she lived in the town? As much as he was looking forward to seeing the guys and celebrating, having this spacious place to himself for a day or two would be a real treat after the relatively confined quarters on *Lady Lydia*.

Phoebe headed for the kitchen. She should have thought to mention the water restrictions before. He'd think she was trying to sneak a peek, coming into the bathroom like that. Too bad. She'd had no choice. The town water situation was critical. He should understand, anyway. On a yacht the water would be rationed.

She'd better text Lindy that one of the best men had arrived safely and everything was fine. Lindy was close to a nervous breakdown as it was, what with Alex sick, the caterers messing her around, and her general attitude of "no one can manage this except me."

Message sent, she put the kettle on to boil and took the plunger coffeepot outside to empty her morning coffee grounds under a tree. What a fabulous view. What a fabulous house. A week there would be luxury after her little cottage. As cozy as it was, it was basically an old-fashioned, unrenovated weatherboard summerhouse. Plus she didn't have to go to work at the bookshop. Imelda was becoming more and more impossible. Always erratic, snappy, and difficult to the point that her staff of two sometimes glumly plotted her murder in a variety of gruesomely elaborate ways, she'd previously left the running of the shop to Phoebe. Now she popped in all the time, checking up on them, finding fault, complaining nonstop.

Maybe Phoebe could find another job before Monday. Where, though? A week or two without a steady income would be the max despite the numerous summer wedding dates she had booked.

Brady's voice startled her. "Beautiful view."

She spun around and nearly dropped the coffeepot. He was clean shaved, refreshed, smiling, dazzling, and stealing her wits away again. In shorts now, he displayed tanned muscular legs. Her eyes flicked up and away. *Mustn't ogle,* she thought.

"Yes."

He took a few expansive breaths. "I miss the smell of the Australian bush. It's quite distinctive."

She dragged her attention away from the rise and fall of his chest. *Say something sensible.* "Have you been away long?" *Good one. Keep it up. Concentrate.*

"I was back here last for Dave's wedding. Three years ago."

"I don't think I'd like to be away from Australia for years." *Going well.*

He shrugged. "I don't have any ties here. I don't really have any ties anywhere," he added with a little laugh.

Now she didn't need to focus her mind to respond. This was a subject she knew all about. Connections were something a person had to work at keeping. According to Lindy, he hadn't wanted ties and had avoided making any, and he didn't sound concerned now about their absence in his life. Phoebe had only the ties she'd painstakingly made herself since Gran had died.

Lindy's parents, Ruth and Phil, were a case in point. She'd deliberately contacted and kept in touch with them when they retired to Narooma. They'd known her parents, or at least her mother. They were a link to that happy time—her roots. The alternative was solitude, leading to loneliness.

"I wouldn't like to live that way."

"How?"

"Not having anyone to care for you, and vice versa."

He said in a careless voice, "I can care for myself. My parents weren't much good at the family thing when they were alive, so I don't miss them, and I'm an only child. I have plenty of friends."

"It's not the same as family, though, is it?" How many times had she wished for siblings during those dark, dismal days after her mother had died suddenly? And later, when she'd lived with a grandmother who had resented the responsibility of caring for an eleven-year-old?

He shrugged. "I don't know. Dave and Alex are the closest thing to brothers I have."

"And now they're both married," she said softly. "Or almost." And their priorities would change. Dave's loyalty had shifted to his wife and their imminent child. Did Brady realize how much his friends' focus would move away from the footloose lifestyles of their youth, leaving him the sole, aging survivor clinging to the rock of his youthful ideals?

Brady laughed. "Poor sods."

"I don't think so. I think they're all incredibly lucky to have found someone who loves them so much and who they love so much. I haven't yet." Thirty-three and still hoping, still searching. Was it so pathetic to want to love and be loved? She shook the empty coffee-pot. Drips of dark brown soggy sludge plopped onto the grass.

"You make it sound inevitable. I like my freedom."

"Dave and Alex are still free. You make marriage sound like a jail term."

"For me it would be. A life sentence."

Phoebe shook her head. Lots of guys made jokes about marriage being a life sentence—she'd heard them all during her years as a celebrant—but Brady was deadly serious. She looked up at his stern profile as he glared across the garden toward the bay. Unbearably attractive he might be, but what he was saying grated on her soul.

"You have a choice in who you marry, you know. It's not a government-assigned pairing off of people. No one forces anyone to marry."

"I know, and I choose not to," he said, with the finality of a locked door.

"Fine, but you can still be happy for your friends who are getting married."

Why was this conversation annoying her so intensely? Why did she care what he thought? Because, she realized, she couldn't bear someone to so blatantly and carelessly dismiss the institution and concept she loved so much—marriage. Not just because she wanted to marry someone, but because she loved the whole idea of caring and sharing and being a family. It was bitterly disappointing, too, that the man who was her physical ideal should think that way.

"Absolutely. Who says I'm not? I came halfway round the world to be here for both of them."

"I should think so." Phoebe turned and stomped up the slope to the steps leading to the deck. What an attitude! Why did he bother coming at all when he held such a blighted view?

"Phoebe." Suddenly, he was beside her, his voice gentle, his hand warm and heavy on her bare arm. "Don't get the wrong idea, please. I'm really happy for both of them. All of them—Alex and Dave and the girls. It's just not my thing."

She looked up. His eyes were gray. Tiny brown and dark blue flecks, invisible from a distance, made them seem darker up close. He smiled, holding her gaze and her arm. His fingers caressed her skin so subtly she could be mistaken, could be imagining some signal he was completely unaware of sending. Whether she was imagining things or not, his touch reignited the lust his earlier attitude had dampened.

"I'm sorry. I'm being rude and obnoxious. My brain's fried." He took the coffeepot from her fingers with his free hand. "Come on. I need a caffeine hit." His fingers slid from her arm, slowly, lazily, and he signaled for her to go ahead.

Phoebe preceded him up the steps, mind whirring, legs wobbling. A safe topic was needed.

"What's your boat called?"

"*Lady Lydia,* and she's a yacht. Charter cruises mostly in the Med or the Caribbean."

"Wow, sounds fantastic. Who's Lydia?"

"I don't know. Maybe the first owner's or builder's wife. Or mistress." He chuckled.

Phoebe paused with her hand on the screen door. She turned. "What do you do on board?"

"I'm the skipper." He reached around her and pulled the screen door open, grinning at her blank-faced astonishment.

"Alex just said you worked on a yacht. He didn't say you were the captain." She stepped inside.

"Skipper of a crew of nine. Not bad for a boy with my background."

"Very impressive. Does Alex know?" What about his background? Alex had never mentioned anything unusual. But men didn't.

"I might not have told him. It's only a recent thing."

Phoebe took the coffeepot and rinsed it out. How amazingly interesting. And how exciting to live on a yacht. No wonder he was hooked on freedom. It'd be hard to give up that life—cruising those exotic places. How dull her life was by comparison.

He sat on a stool at the kitchen bench and watched her take mugs from the shelf, pour hot water into the plunger pot, set milk and sugar and teaspoons out. "Not working at the bookshop today?" he asked.

"No, I took the week off."

"As a holiday?"

"Sort of. I've been thinking of quitting, because the lady who owns the shop is becoming really hard to work for. Very demanding and a bit irrational at times. She accuses us of rifling the till and me of fudging the accounts. I'm the manager, but she comes in all the time, checking up on us and scaring the customers."

He pulled a face. "Not much fun. Do you rifle the till?" The gray eyes studied her, a half smile lurking on those very kissable lips.

She gave a little snort of laughter. "No."

"Is there much work around?"

Her smile faded. "I could find something, I think. I can't afford to be too choosy. I have bills to pay." She glanced at him. "This week, though, I'm bringing in a little more than usual, because friends of a friend jumped at the chance to have my place for the week. Summer holidays at the beach, you see." Phoebe pressed the plunger down. "I'd much rather be here. My place is tiny and old. But I do love it," she added.

"This is certainly a beautiful house." Was he disappointed she was staying here rather than at her own home? It was hard to tell.

"Yes. I need to ask you about your friendship with Alex. For the service. I like to make it very personalized. It's the most important day of their lives." She poured coffee into both mugs. "Even if you don't think so," she added with a tiny smile to show him she was joking—sort of.

"What do you want to know?"

Her phone beeped. "Sorry. That'll be Lindy. I told her you were here."

He nodded. Lindy's text message was brief: *Thanx.*

Phoebe settled herself on the stool next to him. Her knees nearly touched his brown thighs. "I want to know how you met and what your first impressions were of him. Why you liked each other. What annoys you about him. Any little mannerisms and quirky things. That sort of thing. What music he likes. What he enjoys. Food, hobbies."

"Mmm. I'll have to think about it." He took a sip of coffee. "I could tell you about the time we were all thrown in jail, but it might not go down too well."

"Really? Sounds perfect."

He grinned. "It was fun—looking back. We were in Spain and got ourselves mixed up in a street protest by accident. We didn't even know what it was about. Still don't, but the police rounded us up with everyone else. They let us out the next day."

"Anything else?" She picked up her own mug.

"Well, there is the fact that Alex is already married."

Chapter Two

Phoebe nearly fell off the stool. One foot slipped from the rung and hit the floor. Her hand jerked so violently coffee sloshed from the mug, and a steaming river headed for the edge of the bench to drip onto the terra-cotta tiles. She jumped backward out of scalding range.

Brady leaned over and grabbed a dishcloth from the sink. He mopped while she stood gasping, wondering if she'd heard correctly, her mind spinning like a dervish.

"Married? Who to? Why hasn't he said? He must have lied on the marriage license application. Not to mention to Lindy. How could he do that?" The enormity of his statement plummeted to deeper levels of comprehension. "He can't get married on Saturday. I'll have to cancel the wedding."

Brady tossed the dishcloth back onto the draining board. "I doubt whether it was legal, the first one. We were in Acapulco and he fell completely in love with a gorgeous Mexican girl, Juanita. They got themselves married, but then her family found out and Juanita's father came after Alex with an ancient shotgun. We hightailed it out of there, I can tell you."

"But when was that? How long ago?"

He tilted his head, brow furrowed. One hand scratched his chin. "Don't know . . . ten years, twelve maybe."

"Who took the service? A priest?"

"Yes. She wouldn't have a civil ceremony. Come to think of it, that priest was a bit iffy. She said he was her cousin. He may not have been a real priest. I think he was drunk. But then, we were too, so . . ."

17

Phoebe shook her head, trying to clear the nuggets of useful information from the dust and rubble flying about. "What happened to Juanita?"

Brady shrugged. "I don't know."

"Why do you think it's not legal?"

"Since then, I've discovered that in Mexico a religious ceremony isn't legal even if the priest is kosher . . . well, not exactly kosher. You know what I mean. Legit. There has to be a civil ceremony."

"But isn't that irrelevant? Morally, Alex is married to this girl."

"But in all other respects, he isn't and he never was. Her family certainly weren't keen to press the point. The whole affair lasted a day and a half."

"Don't you care?"

Brady stood, hands raised. "Hang on, Phoebe. You're carrying on as if it were me. I didn't marry the girl. I didn't run off and leave her."

"But you were there and you didn't try to stop them." Phoebe glared at him, her hands on her hips.

"How do you know what I did?" His amused smile had gone.

"I can tell."

"How? You've known me an hour at the most." A steely edge entered his voice. His eyes turned darker gray, battleship gray. He was a ship's captain quelling the mutinous crew.

"Your whole attitude is anti-wedding and anti-marriage, and I think you'd be only too happy if this wedding fell through. Why else would you tell me something like that? I'm the celebrant. I have legal responsibilities. And on top of that, the bride's one of my oldest friends." She whirled about and headed for the phone. "I have to talk to Alex."

"No!" Brady strode forward to catch her. "You can't phone him. He's sick. Lindy will answer and then what? Are you going to tell her?"

His hand touched her bare arm, the pressure firm but not intimidating, making her pause, making her think—making her skin tingle. "She needs to know something like that," Phoebe said.

He glared down at her. "Maybe, but not from you. Or me. *He* has to tell her. He might have already." His fingers slipped from her forearm, trailing sparks. Not interested. He probably wanted to throw her in the brig, whatever that was.

"I doubt it. They would've told me. It would've come up when we were doing the paperwork." She screwed her eyes shut and pressed her palms to her face. "What am I going to do?"

"Nothing."

She dropped her hands in amazement, or maybe shock. Brady couldn't seriously mean that, could he? "I can't do *nothing*. They can't start their married life with Alex hiding another wife. Even if she isn't really his wife. It's . . . it's . . . wrong."

He spread his arms and cocked his head in a very French gesture. At least, it looked French. Or Italian. The "What's the problem? And I don't want to get involved" gesture. "Why not? Couples have all sorts of secrets. They lie to each other all the time."

"No, they don't!" He *was* serious. And what sort of people did he mix with? The loose-living, jet-setting Mediterranean yacht owners?

He turned away, muttering, "My parents did. They lied to everyone. Each other, themselves, me, the police."

Phoebe bit her lip. Anger and astonishment subsided rapidly, replaced by a surge of sympathy. This was a different thing altogether. The bitterness in his voice and gesture said it all, an emotional exposure he probably rarely allowed, or was unaware of. "Do you see them, your parents?"

"Nah. Not since I was five." It was gone. The glimpse of another, vulnerable Brady was rapidly obscured by a sneer.

"Who brought you up?"

"A series of foster families." He stared at her. His eyes were cold gray now, windswept and bleak. "Not everyone has a cozy, rosy, happy family background."

"No, that's true. Not everyone does." Least of all her. "But you can't blame marriage for that."

Brady's mouth firmed into a line. He looked for a moment as though he was going to say something more, but instead, he nodded briefly and turned away. The door scraped open, and he stepped onto the sun-drenched wooden verandah outside, a self-contained, emotionally private man, his inner demons subdued and dealt with.

Phoebe hesitated, then headed for the study and the computer. First she needed to check the Mexican marriage legalities. If what Brady had told her regarding civil versus religious ceremonies was true, then that at least wouldn't be an issue. Alex wouldn't legally be a bigamist. Morally was another matter altogether.

But was it her problem or theirs? Complicated, handsome-as-sin Brady was no help at all. And his being so attractive made it worse. What a nightmare.

Brady strode down the slope toward the water glistening between the trees at the perimeter of the property. A narrow path wound from the edge of the grass between the beautiful, tall, straight spotted gums and various shrubby natives. Fallen leaves and twigs crackled underfoot, and he slowed, taking deep breaths of hot fragrant air. A little white wooden jetty came into view as he rounded a curve in the path. A green-painted boat shed was securely locked against intruders, but Brady walked the length of the narrow jetty and stood staring across the bay.

Was Phoebe right? Should the Juanita thing be brought up now? It was a bit late. He'd forgotten all about it, and Alex probably had too. He certainly never mentioned it. Phoebe was overreacting in a typical female way.

"Shouldn't have told her," he muttered. "Fool!" He'd put her into an awkward position as celebrant and legal representative. He hissed, "Idiot!"

But she'd discover what he had: a marriage in Mexico had to be performed by a civil celebrant, or it wasn't recognized as legal. It was never registered anywhere; that was for sure. Was it morally wrong? That was Alex's dilemma, not his or hers. Wasn't it?

Frowning against the glare and the tiresome, brain-wrenching issue his flippant comment had thrown up, Brady turned and walked back to shore. Why couldn't she just leave it alone? Who'd know?

A sleek white seagull screeched overhead and landed on the nearest post, cocking a beady eye his way. A narrow strip of sand stretched away in both directions where the jetty reached land. He turned left, soft white grains squeaking beneath his feet until he reached an impenetrable barrier of rocks and trees forming a little cliff face.

He retraced his steps, becoming more and more conscious of the afternoon sun hammering down on his unprotected head. He had forgotten sunglasses too, and the harshness of the light made his already sore eyes feel even grittier and more uncomfortable. Vicious, the Aussie sun. The shady path back to the house gave welcome relief.

He walked round to the side where his room opened onto the patio. The sliding door was still locked. He'd have to go upstairs and come down from inside. He paused at the steps to the verandah. With any luck Phoebe would still be busy on the computer and he could escape to his room without another confrontation. His brain couldn't cope with any more that day. After a sleep, he'd do better, but it was only a quarter to three. His stomach rumbled and growled as he crossed the spacious living area. When had he eaten last, and which meal had it been?

They'd given him coffee and a biscuit on the Moruya leg, and before that, he'd had breakfast on the international flight, hours earlier. He should have taken Phoebe up on her offer to whip up a meal, instead of snapping at her. He changed tack for the kitchen.

Investigations uncovered plenty of bread, cheese, milk, eggs, fruit, tomatoes and salad vegetables, tins of beans, packets of crackers, and chocolate biscuits. There were heaps of meat in the freezer. No worries! Of course Lindy would have made sure there was plenty of food in readiness to feed eight for the week.

He took four eggs, the cheese, tomatoes, garlic, an onion, and a zucchini and began assembling an omelet, whistling softly under his breath as he worked.

"Smells good." She stood smiling at him but with a distance not evident earlier. The open friendliness had gone. She was being polite. He'd scared her with his savage attack on couples and his disregard for marriage, a social convention that she regarded, albeit innocently and naively, as a desirable state. "I would have cooked something for you."

She was sweet and pretty and deserved better. He gave her his best and friendliest smile, waved the spatula in a little arc. "Sorry, I only just realized I was hungry. Are you? Do you want some?"

"No, thanks. I'll wait for dinner."

She opened the fridge and removed a jug of chilled water. "Would you like a glass?"

"Yes, please." The casual, happy girl was gone, her movements stiff and self-conscious. *Drat!* She was still cross and wary. Why couldn't she let it go?

Phoebe poured two glasses, refilled the jug, and put it back into the fridge with a shaking hand. This man was plain gorgeous, plus he was house-trained. What more could a girl want in a prospective partner? Morals? Depended on the goal. If it was permanency and marriage, Brady was not on the radar. There were too many issues to deal with. If it was a fun, flirtatious week, he most definitely was.

His omelet smelled delicious. Give him two points for cooking ability.

"What do you do on your yacht?"

"We take people out for a couple of weeks sailing around the Caribbean or the Mediterranean or wherever we happen to be at the time. Charters."

"Wow!"

He laughed. "Yes, it is a bit like that."

"Have you been to Cuba?"

"Yep."

"I've always wanted to go to Havana." Hot salsa music swirling in sultry air. Flashing eyes; colored skirts; curvy women showing long tanned legs, dancing with darkly handsome Latin lovers; adventure; romance.

"Nothing stopping you, is there?"

"Hah. Nothing except money."

He nodded. "Money. Always the problem." He switched the gas off under his pan.

While he ate, Phoebe sat at the table with him, toying with her glass of water and trying not to stare at the firm line of his jaw and the crinkles that appeared at the corners of his eyes when he laughed. And the lock of hair that flopped across his brow and made him look young instead of like a stern sea captain. "How long have you been doing charters?"

"About two years with *Lady Lydia*. Before that, I crewed for a very wealthy German couple." He paused, then added, "Wilhelm taught me a great deal."

"Where's *Lady Lydia* now?"

"In dry dock in Marseille, having her bottom scraped. It was good timing, this wedding."

"Sounds painful."

"Be worse if she didn't. Imagine having your bottom crusted with barnacles." He grinned and placed his knife and fork neatly in the center of the empty plate. "Aaahh. That feels better."

Phoebe sat up straight. "What would you like to do now?"

He looked at her with an eyebrow raised. The smoothly shaved planes of his cheeks tempted her fingers. "You don't have to entertain me."

"I know, but you're a visitor and I'm a local. I thought you might like to drive around and see the town, or the beach, or . . . whatever you like," she finished feebly, under the crushing weight of his gaze and the half smile that looked like a smirk. Why would he want to drive around sleepy seaside Narooma when he was used to exotic places like Havana and the French Riviera? She picked up his plate and the empty water glasses.

"You don't have to wait on me either."

"I know. I don't have to do anything for you, but I was trying to be helpful and friendly and make you feel at home after your rotten trip."

She strode to the kitchen and dumped the dishes into the sink. Unaccustomed anger bubbled to the surface. Annoyance at his air of superiority coupled with an uncomfortable and embarrassing feeling that she might have been the tiniest bit obvious in her desire to please this attractive man. He could have any exotic woman he wanted, and most likely did.

He sighed—just loudly enough for her to hear. Phoebe screwed up her mouth, kept her back turned. Insufferably patronizing so-and-so, sitting there thinking what a silly, unsophisticated woman she was, and weren't women difficult and touchy, and didn't the poor blokes have to be careful what they said or everything got blown out of proportion?

"I'm sorry." Chair legs rasped on tiles as he stood up. Hair prickled on the back of her neck as his footsteps came closer. She swallowed a rush of nervous saliva.

"I'm still being rude, aren't I?" He sounded tired, not patronizing.

She turned and got the full force of repentant gray eyes, half-smiling lips.

"It's all right." Now her mouth and throat were parched.

"Maybe a drive round town would be the thing. Keep me awake."

Phoebe nodded. "Fine. If you like." She opened the dishwasher and shoved the plate into a rack, causing a rattle of cutlery.

"I do."

She smiled at the solemnly voiced vow and glanced up with a dirty glass poised.

He laughed. "Guess you've heard that a lot."

"Yes." Her eyes flickered to his and then away. She closed the dishwasher. "I'll lock the house."

He was in the way, lounging against the bench, cornering her, making no attempt to move. She hesitated. If she pushed by, parts of her body would rub on parts of his. Her body would press against his chest; bare arms would touch bare arms; bare thighs would . . . He extended a tanned finger, featherlight, and brushed something from her cheek, scorching a trail. She froze as heat rushed to her face. He smiled.

"Bit of fluff," he said. He folded his arms comfortably, still lounging, still blocking her path, watching, waiting, smiling. "Are we going?"

"Yes. Lock those sliding doors, will you, please?" She waited for him to unfold his arms and heave his lanky frame away from the bench. He did, slowly, still wearing a knowing grin. She was so obvious! He was a cat and she was the mouse—a mouse who screamed "Come and get me" from every pore.

Phoebe darted through the widened gap and headed for the other end of the house, where she managed to regroup while closing and locking windows.

She drove to the main street, then turned for the beach. The little parking area was crowded, but she squeezed the Beetle into a tiny space. Brady managed to open the door enough to crawl out of his bucketlike seat and squirm between the two cars.

"You can back it out first when we leave; then I'll get in," he said.

"Good idea. Like an ice cream?" She pointed to the surf club building, where signboards, colored flags, and a knot of scantily clad people clustered round an open window indicated a snack bar.

"No, thanks." The cold would attack that aching tooth with a vengeance. If anything, it was getting worse.

"I'm having one." A cheery smile came his way. She was happy again. *Good*. She didn't hold a grudge. Women who held grudges, real or imaginary, were the pits.

She queued with a couple of young boys and a handful of frazzled parents with cranky toddlers. He walked to where the rough grass met golden sand, and inhaled a deep, lung-cleansing draft of salt-laden air. *Beautiful*. He'd forgotten how clean and clear the air was down here. The horizon, a choppy line of darker blue fading into the sky, was visible in the heat haze. Seagulls squawked and swirled overhead, occasionally dive-bombing prospective food providers. It was the same the world over.

The wide beach stretched in both directions, dotted with sunbathers sitting under colored umbrellas or lying on towels; children running; swimmers splashing in the surf, laughing and shouting. The lifeguards' yellow and red flags fluttered gaily from the poles set up to the left. A chalkboard gave wind direction, currents, water temperature, and surf conditions. That day there was a light wind, a strong southerly rip, and a water temperature of seventy-three degrees.

"Lovely, isn't it?" Phoebe appeared beside him, licking a double-scoop chocolate cone.

"Yes. It hasn't changed."

"Did you come here for holidays?"

"Not here exactly. One family took me to the beach—I forget which—for a holiday once." He kept his gaze on the distant horizon. An island lay offshore to their right. The hazy bulk of a tanker slid slowly by, its superstructure just visible above the line of waves. "I loved it."

"The sea?"

"Yes. I wanted to run away to sea."

He glanced at her. She didn't reply, busy with her ice cream, which was melting almost faster than she could lick. Chocolate blobbed onto her chin. What would she do if he licked it off, slid his tongue over that smooth skin, moved upward to her lips, kissed her? He looked away.

"So you decided to become a sailor because of that holiday?"

He strode down the slope onto the sand. Was she laughing at him? Laughing at the dream of a little boy to sail off into the vastness of the ocean and never come back? He'd never told anyone he'd wanted to be a sailor from the age of nine—not even Alex and Dave, his best mates. Why tell this woman? He slipped his sandals off and walked toward the incoming wash of waves.

Phoebe was by his elbow, pink cheeked under her straw sun hat. She bit hugely into the ice cream and giggled, cheeks bulging.

"Whoops!" came out in a smothered gurgle.

"I suppose you think that's stupid," he said.

"No, not at all." She held the remains of the cone in her mouth, took off her shoes, and rolled the legs of her pants up over her knees, then straightened and recommenced eating. She swallowed. "I love the sea too. That's why I stayed here when . . ." The hesitation and suddenly subdued tone made him frown.

"When what?"

He slowed his pace to suit hers, walking on wet, hard sand on the edge of the incoming arcs of froth.

"My gran died." A finger wiped delicately at the corners of her mouth.

"Did you live with your grandmother?" That was a surprise. If he'd thought about it, he would have pegged her as a girl with a nice set of middle-class parents in a comfortable suburban house. A couple of siblings and a dog for good measure.

"Since I was eleven. She retired down here when I was about twenty, but when she had a stroke, I moved from Canberra to care for her."

"What happened to your parents?"

"My father died in a workplace accident when I was four. He was a builder and some scaffolding collapsed. Mum died of an aneurysm seven years later. It was very sudden. Both of them."

He frowned. He hadn't expected that. Not at all. "I'm sorry. Do you have brothers and sisters?"

"No. Just me." She wasn't bitter, didn't sound sad—just accepting.

"You were lucky your grandmother took you in."

Phoebe didn't reply, but he sensed a reaction. She slowed, her head angled so the hat covered his view of her face. He stood in front of her and peered underneath it, lifting the brim with one hand. She stopped and looked at him, had no choice. Her mouth still had traces of chocolate at the corners. Dark glasses hid her eyes. What color were they? He hadn't noticed.

"What?" he asked softly. A wave sloshed about their ankles, tugging at the sand under his feet.

"She didn't think so." Her mouth trembled.

Brady lifted the hat from her head, didn't think, didn't rationalize, acted on impulse. He leaned forward and pressed his lips on hers, all soft and yielding and sweet, tasting of chocolate. She gave a small gasp and lurched as the next wave ripped the sand from under them both. He drew back, stepped away a pace onto firmer ground. Was she annoyed? He couldn't tell. He'd better not do that again. It was too tempting, way too addictive. He licked his lips and tasted chocolate. Sweet, sweet, innocent Phoebe.

"You taste of chocolate," he said, stupid from confusion and whirling hormones.

She smiled. She wasn't angry. He couldn't read her eyes through the glasses. She wouldn't be able to read his either. Lucky that, because she'd see desire and shock, a total lack of self-control, shaky vulnerability.

"Why did you do that?" She sounded more curious than anything. She took her hat from his hand and jammed it onto her head.

"I like kissing pretty girls." It was his standard response. Legs on automatic, he began walking back the way they'd come. She kept pace. "And you looked sad. I wanted to cheer you up." Why had he done that? He wanted to, most of all, but she wasn't the flirtatious girl he'd originally thought she was. He would be in Australia for only a week. Nothing could develop here.

"Thanks."

"Did you mind?" He cocked an eyebrow at her.

"No. It was a nice kiss."

Nice? Nice was the kiss of death. "Thanks."

She chuckled softly and walked farther left so the waves washed around her ankles.

"Why didn't your grandmother want you to stay?" he called over the crash of an incoming curler.

She shrugged. He joined her in water that alternated between ankle- and knee-deep, cool and refreshing to overheated blood. "She had her own life. There wasn't room for a child in it. She felt she'd done her bit raising her own kids."

"So you have uncles and aunts." He didn't, as far as he knew. None who wanted to claim him, anyway. Not a soul in the world wanted him as kin.

"A bachelor uncle who's a bit odd, and an aunt and uncle in Darwin with three kids of their own and no room for me. Mum was an only child, and her parents couldn't take me. They'd moved up north to a retirement village."

"So we're the same in some ways," he said slowly. "Nobody wanted us."

"I suppose we are. Although . . ."

Two kids darted past, laughing and shoving each other. Phoebe stopped to avoid a collision. An overweight father jogged after the boys, yelling at them to be careful.

"Families aren't what they're cracked up to be." Brady said it without any particular intention of reigniting the earlier argument, but her voice turned as cold as her ice cream.

"And that's where we differ."

Phoebe splashed into deeper water. Her pant legs were wet, but who cared? Brady Winters sure didn't waste any time when he spied one of his "pretty girls." He'd kissed her after how many hours' acquaintance? About three or four at most. If she was up for something more intimate, he certainly was. And that was very, very disappointing— surprisingly disappointing. Especially now that she'd begun to understand his antipathy toward family, to feel sympathy for him for what must have been a very tough childhood. He'd fulfilled her original expectations of a worldly-wise, confident man on the make, a magnificently good-looking dream of a man with the sex drive of a tomcat and the morals to go with it. Not a man driven by an intense desire to kiss her, Phoebe Curtis. Any pretty girl would do.

Thank goodness she'd been surprised enough not to react in time, able to pretend indifference and mild enjoyment rather than show the melted mess she really was the instant his lips touched hers, able to pretend that her sagging knees were caused by waves and shifting sand rather than complete muscle failure, able to bring him down with a beautifully timed "nice." The look on his face had been framable.

At least she knew now exactly where she stood and could plan her reactions accordingly. *Cool* would be the watchword. When the others arrived, everything would change: the dynamics would shift, and the three best mates would revert to rough-and-tumble boy stuff. All she had to do was survive until they turned up on Wednesday. The effects of Brady would be diluted.

"Can we go home via your shop?"

"Why?" The shop? Talk about non sequiturs. She looked at him splashing beside her. He must have guessed the extent of her surprise. It was the last place she wanted to go.

"I haven't got anything to read. I finished my book on the plane."

"What do you read?" *Right*. Kisses forgotten, Phoebe was filed away as a lost cause, a DON'T BOTHER sign plastered on her forehead in his mind.

"Action. International intrigue. Clive Cussler, Wilbur Smith. I like a good murder too."

"Don't we all."

He laughed. "I bet you read romance."

"And why not?" She loved romances, but forensic crime was a favorite at the moment.

He held up his hands in mock defense. "No reason. I've read *Pride and Prejudice* and *Wuthering Heights*."

"Really?"

"Had to at school."

She bent and flicked a handful of water at him, wetting her sandals. Brady sprinted onto dry land.

"Coward," she called, but she joined him in trudging through soft hot sand between children, towels, umbrellas, and comatose sun-baking bodies, heading for the parking area.

"You're already half soaked, and I'm too much of a gentleman to dunk you completely."

"I'll bet."

"We should come for a swim tomorrow."

"So you can dunk me?" Exploratory flirting was over. He'd moved on to friends—which was to be expected.

"Never." He laughed.

Phoebe parked the Beetle a few doors from Imelda's Preloved Books.

"I'll wait here," she said.

Brady paused with the door open and one foot on the pavement. He looked over his shoulder, brow wrinkled. "Come with me."

"No. I'm on holiday. I don't want to go in there."

A little grin twisted his lips. "Are you scared of the boss?"

"No." Imelda might not be there, but on the other hand, odds were high she was. Phoebe really didn't want to deal with any accusations and bizarre rants. This was her holiday!

"Come with me, then. I want your expert advice and a discount."

"We don't give discounts." Heaven knows what would happen if they did that. The sky might fall.

"Come on. I'll protect you." He bounded from the car and slammed the door. Phoebe hesitated. What was she worried about? Imelda should be pleased she was bringing in a customer. She'd given her approval for the week off, and it was Phoebe's right to take holidays.

She joined him, reluctantly, on the footpath.

"Coward," he said.

"I'm not. It's just that I was looking forward to getting away from the place. I didn't want to come straight back in on my first day off."

"We'll be ten minutes. Less. I make up my mind very quickly. Zip in and out and she'll never know you've been." He gave a confident little chuckle and pushed the door open. The Swiss cowbell jangled. Imelda's ears would be twitching.

"Moo," he murmured.

Phoebe snorted with laughter despite the heavy sag in her stomach. Three or four customers browsed the crammed shelves. Gavin and Imelda weren't in sight, but Imelda's cockatoo-like screeching voice carried through from the rear of the shop. She had only one volume level: eleven.

"I've asked you many times not to stack books like that, Gavin. Don't you people ever listen?" Poor Gavin. If there weren't two of them working there, supporting each other and diffusing the attack, they'd go nuts.

Heavy footsteps pounded the bare wooden floor toward the front counter. The cowbell and its promise of customers drew Imelda like a magnet. She charged along in her sensible shoes and habitual floral-print dress like a wayward flower cart. Phoebe grabbed Brady's arm and dragged him down the closest aisle. Biography, autobiography, travel, maps and geography.

"I don't want any of this," he said loudly. "Where's general fiction?"

She lowered her voice. "Center aisle." She never should have let him talk her into coming in. Now they'd have to run the gauntlet of Imelda before they could leave. He had no idea.

He studied Phoebe with an exaggerated expression of puzzlement. "What is *wrong* with you? You really are scared of the woman, aren't you? Don't be so ridiculous." He took her hand and pulled her along to the front of the shop. They burst into the small patch of open space in front of the overstacked counter, with Brady already wheeling round to dive down the center aisle, towing her reluctant body.

"Phoebe!" Imelda glared through heavy-duty glasses. They magnified her eyes to alarming pools of washed-out blue under her iron-gray fringe of hair. "You told me you were going away to a friend's wedding."

Brady stopped and turned. Phoebe stumbled into his chest. He steadied her. She pulled her hand from his and faced her accuser, who had, as usual, made up her own version of the facts. Confrontation was useless. Patience was essential. Calm reiteration of the truth was best. A smile would be good but was impossible to manage at the moment.

"I didn't say I was going away. I said a friend was getting married."

Imelda sniffed, which indicated extreme disapproval, way beyond the usual medium-level disapproval with which she viewed everything. "But you're obviously still here. You told a lie. I wouldn't have given you the time off if I'd known you weren't going away."

Curious customers edged closer, pretending to browse, ears flapping. Gavin's anxious face hovered moonlike in the background next to shelves of Fiction—Historical. Brady gave a soft snort, which could have been laughter. She didn't dare look at him with her face pulsating with overheated blood, and with her anger at his deliberate denseness rising like milk on the boil.

"Imelda, I didn't lie. I asked for a week off to go to a wedding, and you agreed."

"It's our busiest time of the year; you know that. You deliberately misled me, and that's absolutely unforgivable after the trust I've put in you. I can't abide liars." Her mouth twisted into a familiar shape— chook's bum, Gavin called it. "And now you come waltzing in with that brazen face, thinking I won't mind. Well, I do!"

"I think you're being very unfair," Brady said. He smiled. Charm wouldn't work on Imelda; he needn't bother trying.

"And who are you?" The firing squad gaze swung to him.

"Brady Winters. I'm a friend of Phoebe's." He held out his hand, still employing the playboy charm. He didn't get it at all. Imelda wasn't just immune; she was actively anti-charm.

The foghorn voice announced to the fascinated bystanders triumphantly, "I see what's going on here. Phoebe took time off to play around with her boyfriend. I doubt whether there even *is* a friend or a wedding."

"No way!" This was monstrous and over-the-top even for Imelda on a bad day. "You gave me a week's leave, which I'm entitled to."

"Entitled you may be, but you don't even have the consideration to ask for it in a quiet time of the year. I put myself out to accommodate you, and this is what I find. You're having an affair with a man." The last word was delivered with all the venom of a bitter woman whose marriage had ended badly, never to be forgotten or forgiven.

Phoebe gasped and someone giggled explosively behind her. Brady's voice cut through the whispering and *shhh*ing.

"And what if she is? It's no one's business what she does on her holidays. Certainly not yours. I can't imagine why Phoebe would want to work for someone like you."

"Brady. Don't."

She tugged at his arm, but he continued in his captain's voice, "I've never met a ruder person in my life, and I've met some right shockers in my time at sea. Phoebe can do far better than work here, and I'm surprised she puts up with it. Him too." He nodded at Gavin, who ducked out of sight. "I'm surprised you can keep staff at all. If I treated my crew that way, there'd be mutiny, and rightly so."

Imelda glared at Phoebe. "Well, if that's the way you feel about the position of trust and importance I've given you, you needn't bother coming back."

Phoebe opened her mouth to say she didn't feel that way, but Brady spoke for her—again.

"She won't." He grabbed her arm and virtually frog-marched her out the door. At the doorstep he paused. "And if she has any wages owing, you'd darn well better see she gets paid. Or there'll be trouble."

Outside, down the footpath a few meters, he released his hold on her arm and burst out laughing. "That sorted the old bat out. What a monster."

Phoebe stood openmouthed in astonishment, limbs and brain frozen by shock.

"You lost me my job," she finally managed to blurt.

"Looks like it. Let's go and celebrate."

Chapter Three

He looked up and down the street, hands on hips, the pleased grin still plastered on his face. "There's a place. Let's go there." He pointed at O'Riley's hotel, down and across the street, boasting a million-dollar view from its expansive terrace.

"No! There's nothing to celebrate. I need that job. I have to go back and apologize." She whirled around, but Brady's hand snaked out and grasped hers firmly again.

"No, you don't."

The shop door opened with a clang of cowbell, and two young women came out giggling. They glanced toward them before they sauntered away, leaving a trail of laughter in the hot air.

"Leave me alone!" Phoebe's eyes flashed lightning.

He tightened his grip despite her fury. "No. You're not going to go back in there and grovel to that woman. Have some self-respect."

"That's easy for you to say. You're only here for a week. You have a job working for millionaires on the Riviera. I don't. I'm here in Narooma trying to survive."

"You can find another job. A better one."

Her eyes narrowed, but she stopped struggling and stepped closer to glare into his face. *Brown,* her eyes were brown, like melted chocolate. "Oh yeah? Where?"

"There must be plenty of places." He released his hold on her fingers, reluctantly, fighting the urge to toss out the old "Gee, you're pretty when you're angry" cliché. But she *was* pretty—and very angry. He wanted to kiss her. She snatched her hand away and folded her arms.

"You find me a job, then."

Brady licked his lips. *Cripes!* She was serious. "You said you could find another job fairly easily."

"You've got till next Monday." Her eyes stayed glued to his face, unwavering, furious.

"I leave on Sunday."

"You've got until Saturday, then. And if I don't have a job that I like and that pays an equal or better wage by Saturday, you have to go in there and apologize to Imelda, tell her it was all your fault, and beg her to give me my job back." She paused, then added, "Convince her to give me my job back."

Brady sucked in air through taut lips. The chances of that last happening were as good as Imelda's chances of becoming a Playboy Bunny. How hard could it be? Buy a copy of the paper, make a few phone calls, and Phoebe would have herself a new job in no time. There must be plenty of waitressing jobs and shop assistant positions open for the summer.

"I don't see why you're so upset. You said yourself you were thinking of changing jobs because the old bat was mad."

"Thinking! Thinking of changing jobs. There's a subtle difference there." She flung her arms wide and stomped toward the Beetle. Brady followed. They were not going to the bar, apparently. He was parched.

"Don't you want to go for a drink?" he asked hopefully. "Drown your sorrows?"

She shook her head as she opened the car door. "You can go. Or there's beer at home."

"I'll come home with you." He threw the passenger door open and jumped in, in case she thought a long walk would do him good or he'd worn out his welcome already. He sighed.

Phoebe's eyes never strayed from the road ahead. She changed gears, indicated turns, braked, accelerated, all with grim determination and tight, furious movements. She was nothing like the carefree, excited, happy girl who'd picked him up that morning, or the one slurping ice cream on the beach, the one he'd kissed. It was his fault.

"Sorry," he said.

"Too late for sorry."

"I still think you're better off."

"You would," she muttered with an infuriatingly dismissive intonation.

"Why would I in particular?" Any fledgling feelings of guilt were swamped by a wave of annoyance. Who did she think she was?

"You only think in terms of yourself. You think, 'What would be best for me?' and then assume it's best for everyone else. You're a supreme egotist."

"And you've known me exactly how long?" he fired at her, stung. He'd heard those accusations before.

"Exactly as long as you've known me," came ripping back. "And yet you presumed you knew what I wanted in terms of my job. How dare you interfere? How do you know what I really want? You don't know anything about our lives here, my life. How do you know Imelda isn't ill and we don't put up with her rantings because she has a terminal condition? A brain tumor."

"Does she?" That possibility had *never* entered his head.

"Not as far as I know, but then, neither did you when you launched your attack."

"I'm sorry."

"So am I."

She drove the rest of the way in steaming silence.

Phoebe stood in the bathtub, rinsing residual sand from her feet and legs, focusing hard on the task and using a minimal amount of water. If she allowed her thoughts to waver, they'd go straight to Brady, and fury would overwhelm her with such force she couldn't hold herself accountable. Of course, it was virtually impossible not to think about him. He'd catapulted her life into turmoil the moment she'd laid eyes on his handsome face.

Being disablingly attractive was the starter, but then he negated that by deriding her belief in marriage and family. Confiding his childhood dream swung the sympathy pendulum back again, but kissing her added more confusion. Was he attracted to her, or was he simply after some action?

Then, to complete the emotional whirlwind of an afternoon, he'd lost her her job. That was more devastating than any of the preceding. And he didn't seem to care!

What sort of man was he?

She yanked the lever to open the drain. So much for good-looking men—totally full of themselves. Lindy was right about him. He had no sense of responsibility—or at least he was responsible only insofar as he and presumably his precious boat were affected. *Unbelievable. A pox upon him! May barnacles encrust his bottom and maggots infest his sea rations.*

Growling and muttering dire nautical-inspired curses under her breath, Phoebe dried her feet and pulled on clean white Capri pants. When she entered the kitchen, he was busy at the bench, back turned so she couldn't see what he was doing. He opened the fridge and took something out.

"Like a cold drink?" he asked, smiling that dazzling and oh-so-charming smile—hoping to smarm his way out of trouble. She could do civilized. She'd had plenty of practice with Imelda and customers in the shop.

"Thanks. I'll have a glass of iced juice."

A cloth-covered bowl sat on the bench. The chopping board, a knife, garlic peels, olive oil, a squeezed lemon, and a bottle of red wine were strewn about.

"Coming right up."

She indicated the mess. "What are you doing?"

"Marinating our steaks before I barbecue them." He handed her a glass of juice with ice tinkling against the sides and gave her another stunner of a smile. "I thought a barbecue would be easy tonight. There's plenty of meat in the fridge."

Phoebe took the glass. "Thanks," she said with no smile. She couldn't do smiling yet.

"Sit down and enjoy it. I'll take care of dinner. Do they have any music here?"

"Yes. Mostly classical." It wasn't her favorite, but it was bearable. He'd hate it. He liked the Rolling Stones and had a tattoo—maybe more than one. Forcing her thoughts away from where other tattoos might lurk, she walked to the stereo system and studied the CD collection. Only a few names were familiar: Beethoven, Bach, Vivaldi, Mozart. Mozart might soothe her and annoy him. She pulled one out at random—*Opera Favorites: Mozart Arias*. Perfect.

She slid the CD into the player, pressed buttons, and wandered out to sit on the verandah with an orchestra revving up in the living room. Let him do dinner. Let him clean up the mess he was making. Let him do everything. He owed her big-time.

Brady appeared and placed a plate on the little cane table next to her. Cheese cubes, olives, almonds, salami, crackers, a little tub of dip, and potato chips.

"Antipasto," he said. "Not brilliant but the best I could do with what's in stock."

She licked her lips. It was not going to be easy staying angry. He was an expert defuser of tension. But then, he'd probably had a lot of practice soothing furious rich women. She took a cheese cube. He dragged up another of the comfortable green-and-white-striped cushioned outdoor chairs and sat next to her. He settled back, nursing his drink and crunching chips.

"Lovely evening," he said, and exhaled deeply. "So peaceful."

A soprano trilled and soared behind them. She was quite penetrating, especially when she hit those high notes. Phoebe ate an olive to hide her smile. This would test how far his guilt-fueled politeness stretched.

"Mmm." A soft, warm breath of air, heavy with the salty smell of the sea, caressed her face. Gum trees rustled gently on the far side of the garden. A couple of birds chortled and warbled somewhere in the branches, singing along with the piping soprano voice. Phoebe leaned her head back and closed her eyes. This could have been the perfect start to a week of fun and relaxation. It should have been perfect. If only she was on holiday instead of unemployed . . .

If it wasn't for Brady and his confident, insensitive, loud mouth . . . She forced her jaw to unclench. *Think of something else. Breathe deeply. Calm.* This singing would be boring into his jet-lagged head like a dentist's drill. *Nice choice.*

" 'Queen of the Night,' " he said.

"Pardon?" Her eyes flicked open. He sounded pleased. Appreciative, even.

"This aria. It's the 'Queen of the Night' from *The Magic Flute.*"

"Oh." She hadn't looked at track titles.

"It's very well known." He sucked on his beer. "Very difficult."

"Mmm." The voice bounced between notes with bell-like precision. "She's good." Amazing singing, now that she listened properly.

"Yes." Brady sat forward, head inclined to hear better, a slight furrow on his brow. "It sounds like Petronella Verkouter. Is it?"

Phoebe gulped back her surprise. He knew the singer? "I don't know."

"She sailed with us a few years ago. Lovely Dutch lady." He sat back, smiling, gazing out across the trees and the bay to the distant blue-hazed mountains with a faraway look on his face.

Phoebe sighed, drank more juice, and gave up. He was more experienced, more worldly, more everything than she was. She had no way of outsmarting him. All she could do was hope he found her a job before he left and, when he did leave, hope he never came back.

Her mobile phone chirruped from the table inside. She glanced at her watch. It was nearly six-thirty. It'd be an aghast and horrified Gavin, for sure.

"Excuse me."

Gavin calling was on the little screen. Phoebe pressed TALK and turned so she had a view out to the verandah and Brady—so she could give him the evil eye.

"Hi, Gavin."

"Phoebe! What happened today? Who was that guy?" He'd be beside himself with shock.

"He's a best man at the wedding. Remember I said the groom has his two best mates? Well, this is one of them. I picked him up at the airport today."

Brady leaned forward and scraped a cracker in the dip with not a care in the world.

"Maybe you should have left him there."

"My sentiments entirely."

Brady stuck his feet up on the railing, drained the beer, and carefully put the bottle down by his side.

"Imelda nearly had a heart attack after you left. She went all purple and shaky. I've never seen her so angry. I don't think you'd better show your face for a while."

"I won't; don't worry. She fired me, remember?" Brady's head turned slightly. He was eavesdropping. She didn't care.

"But she'll probably take you back after she calms down. She won't find anyone else willing to put up with her."

Phoebe licked salt tang from her lips, considering the statement. "No." And maybe Brady was right. Why should she put up with that treatment?

"If you apologize enough, she'll come round." Anxious Gavin was trying to smooth over the rift, reestablish the status quo. He hated confrontation and nastiness in any form, which was why he'd hidden behind the shelves and hadn't supported her and had always made her deal with difficult customers.

Phoebe frowned. Why should she apologize to Imelda rather than the other way round? If apologies were to be made, Brady should kick them off. And come to think of it, he *had* apologized on the way home.

"But I didn't do anything wrong. She gave me the time off. You were there. You know I didn't lie."

"I know, but we know how she is."

Not good enough. "I'm sick of being accused of stuff, Gavin. Aren't you? We shouldn't have to put up with that rubbish. I don't want to come back."

"What are you going to do?"

She lowered her voice and turned her back to the verandah. "Brady—the guy—is finding me another job. I was so angry with him for interfering I made him promise to find me one before he leaves, or grovel to Imelda and get my old one back."

Gavin laughed. "Good for you! When's he leaving?"

"Sunday." She giggled.

"You'll be waitressing at the Tavern."

"I don't like waitressing and no way will I serve beer to drunken yobbos at a place like that. I told him I wanted something I like and with equal or better money."

"Well, good luck."

"How will you manage on your own with Imelda?"

"Okay. I just keep quiet and agree with everything she says." That was his problem.

"I'll let you know what happens. Thanks for calling, Gavin."

"I was worried about you."

"Thanks. I'm fine. I'll be fine."

She disconnected and stood for a moment watching Brady through the open doorway. He'd sunk back into the chair with one ankle balanced on the other knee, right arm hanging relaxed over the side.

Had he done her a favor? It was true she'd wanted to change jobs. Gavin could put up with that rubbish if he liked, but she really didn't want to go to work each day expecting to be abused and accused of lying in front of the customers. It was a ridiculous, nerve-racking way to live.

She walked out to the verandah and picked up her glass. Brady was asleep, head lolling, chest rising and falling rhythmically. Did he realize the extent of the havoc he'd caused in her life? Did he care? Her fingers tightened on the glass. Whether she'd wanted to quit was irrelevant. It had been her decision to make, not his. He'd interfered already in her professional capacity as a celebrant, casually dropping that grenade in her lap about Alex's Mexican marriage. Despite the fact that the marriage wasn't legal, the potential for an explosion was still there. She wouldn't tell Lindy, but she was darn well going to have a quiet and not-so-subtle word with Alex about it.

Brady showed no signs of waking. So much for doing the dinner. If they were going to eat soon, she'd have to start the barbecue. She walked down the steps to the little covered area where the gas-fired monstrosity lived along with the outdoor dining furniture. Phil and Ruth had assured her when they'd dropped the keys off the day before that the gas tanks were full; they'd checked when they'd delivered the mass of groceries ordered by Lindy.

All shiny silver and chrome surfaces, this was the biggest, most complicated barbecue Phoebe had ever seen. Her idea of an outdoor cooking appliance was either an open fire with a grill over it or one of those dish-shaped things with coals. Fortunately, someone—probably Phil—had left instructions, clearly typed and in a plastic sleeve taped to the lid, for the barbecue-challenged operators, the ones without a science degree. Lindy had learned her organizational skills from her father.

Phoebe read the directions three times, then carefully turned the required knobs and pressed IGNITION. Something whooshed, and a blue flame burned cheerfully under the griller section. *Very good.* Her hard-won university education had been worthwhile after all, contrary to Gran's opinion.

She returned to the verandah. A slow and beautiful melody was wafting from the CD player now. Brady would know what that was too, probably. She stared down at him, so relaxed in sleep, innocent. A little tug of desire stirred deep inside her. He'd kissed her. She'd wanted him to the instant she'd seen him; she'd never thought he would; she knew he wouldn't do it again. Her moment had gone with the waves running out to sea at the beach.

But those well-constructed features hid a mass of contradictions. Some of his opinions were ugly to her, but he wasn't a nasty or vicious man. He had kindness in there along with the devil-may-care attitude, and a deep sense of loyalty and friendship, evidenced by his willingness to travel halfway round the world to be a best man, and by being asked to be a best man. Twice.

Was everyone else as complex? She wasn't. She was simple, with simple desires and ambitions. Brady would probably say the same thing about himself.

She scooped up the empty beer bottle, stacked the remains of the antipasto on the tray, shook her head at the incomprehensible, and continued to the kitchen. Potato salad would go nicely with the steaks and a salad using Phil's homegrown tomatoes and lettuce. *Easy.*

Brady woke with the tantalizing aroma of barbecuing meat and onions in his nostrils. His stomach growled and gurgled as he stretched his arms overhead and straightened his creaky back. Twenty plus hours of sitting in planes with seats apparently designed for children had made his body feel like an origami sampler. A quick glance at his watch told him he'd been asleep nearly an hour. Mozart had been replaced by Neil Diamond, and the setting sun streamed golden rays into his bleary eyes through the treetops. A wash of evening pinks and purples stained the sky.

He grimaced. If there was one voice he couldn't stand, it was Neil Diamond's. Women loved him, though. Phoebe the romantic was probably a massive fan of the man. Better not spoil the truce by complaining about her choice of music.

She was standing at the barbecue with fork and tongs poised, studying the spluttering steaks. He joined her. How cross would she be now? He'd meant to cook dinner as an atonement of sorts. He'd said she needn't do a thing, and she was doing the lot. He prepared himself for the chill of her resentment.

"Sorry I went to sleep and left you to do this."

She turned, startled. Then she smiled.

A weight lifted from his chest. He must be forgiven—partially, at least. That thought made him glad. He realized he hated being responsible for removing the lovely smile from her face, for causing Phoebe sadness and worry. He wanted her to be happy. Guilt for his rash attack on the Imelda woman made a surprise appearance in his gut. He rarely felt guilty about anything. His actions outside his work life usually affected only him. He'd better send her some flowers with a note the next day.

"It's fine. You can't fight jet lag. I was a bit worried about blowing us up, but Phil left detailed instructions." She pointed to a plastic-covered page lying on one of the wooden benches. "It was taped to the lid, but I thought it might melt."

"I was going to bake potatoes in foil. Too late now. Sorry."

"It's okay. I made potato salad and a green salad."

He sighed. "Struck out all round. My turn tomorrow. I'll take you out to dinner."

"Lovely. We can celebrate my new job," she said sweetly.

"Have you found one already?" Hope flared. Was that why she was smiling?

"No. That's your job. I'm thinking positively."

"Right." He watched her flip onion rings. "Nearly ready? I'll set the table."

"Two minutes."

Brady strode to the verandah steps. Neil Diamond's thick voice howled from the living room. If he ate with that going, he'd get indigestion. He paused. "Mind if I change the CD?"

Phoebe turned. "Don't like him?"

"Do you?"

She tilted her head with a tiny smile. "I thought you might."

"I'm not a fan, no."

"Put something else on. You choose this time."

He bounded up the steps and silenced the grating, tuneless noise with a flick of the wrist. Did she like Neil Diamond or not? She hadn't answered. He scanned the shelf. The owners were classical buffs. There wasn't much else except for several more Neil Diamond albums, Barbra Streisand, and *Broadway Showstoppers*. What an aberration in taste. It was a toss-up which was worst. Silence would be preferable. He turned the player off.

When Phoebe carried the steaks and onions piled on a platter up the steps and into the dining area, the long table was set with two places at one end. Two clean glasses stood waiting with a jug of iced water and two bowls of salad.

"Looks good," he said, as she carefully set the platter on a cork place mat.

"Help yourself." She sat down. He hadn't put any music on, which was a relief. The next day she'd nip home and collect some of her own CDs, and if he didn't like her taste, then tough. Neil Diamond had been a near success. Brady obviously didn't like him but was too polite to say so, which nearly made her laugh. But if he hadn't suggested changing the CD, she would have had to race up and change it herself. The man's voice set her teeth on edge. Thank goodness Brady had woken up after only two tracks.

He poured water into both glasses and lifted his. She raised hers, and he clinked it, looking her in the eye. "Santé."

"Cheers."

He held her gaze over the rim of his glass. "Please can we be friends, Phoebe?"

She sipped. *Friends?* They didn't have much in common. Too much emotional turmoil surrounded her impressions of him for her to separate what was what. There was no point being awkward and difficult, though, when they were sharing a house, and extra tension would ruin Lindy's wedding plans. "I'm sure we can manage that. For the rest of the week."

"If I try really hard," he said with a grimace. "I didn't start off very well, did I?"

"No. You were appallingly bad." She scooped potato salad onto her plate and handed him the spoon.

He dolloped himself a large helping. "I'll start job hunting tomorrow. What do you really want to do?"

"What do you mean?"

"Don't you have a dream job? Something you've always wanted to do? Like I wanted to be a sailor. This steak is great, by the way. Good marinade." He grinned and sawed off another chunk.

Phoebe speared a piece of lettuce and ate it, pondering his question. She had no passion for any particular career. He'd laugh and scoff if she told him her real life dream—to be someone's wife and have children, create a happy, loving family and a safe haven, a home. Women were supposed to be career oriented these days. "I liked working in the bookshop. I like meeting people. I hate waitressing, though. Don't even think about waitressing jobs." She frowned at him.

"Promise," he said.

"There's not much else around, you realize."

"There must be something." His brow was creased now, gray eyes shadowed with doubt. The reality of the situation must be finally sinking in. He was chewing his steak slowly and thoughtfully.

"And I don't want to drive to the next town every day, so don't consider Moruya or Bega or somewhere like that."

That shook him. He put his fork down and drank some water. The frown deepened. Visions of apologizing to Imelda would be the stuff of nightmares to a man like Brady. "You're making it rather restrictive."

"I had a job that filled all those requirements." Phoebe met his irritated gaze with calm detachment. "I want another one."

"I'll do my best."

She sliced off a piece of her steak. It was good, tender and juicy with a nice flavor from his marinade. Brady wouldn't be enjoying his as much with the prospect of groveling to Imelda hanging over his head. It served him right. An uncontrollable little burst of laughter made her snort into her dinner.

"What are you laughing about?"

"Nothing."

"Tell me."

"Looks like you'll be apologizing to Imelda on Friday."

His eyes narrowed. "Don't be so sure."

She smiled and raised her glass to him. "Good luck."

He leaned forward, suddenly serious. "Phoebe, what do you really want out of life?"

Startled by the intensity of his gaze and the switch of mood, she lowered her glass, bit her lower lip gently. "You'll laugh," she said softly.

He shook his head. "I won't. I don't laugh at dreams."

His eyes were gentle, interested, swallowing her up. She plunged in. What did it matter? He was here for six days, in and out of her life like a whirlwind.

"I want to marry someone. I want to have children. I want to be part of a family, create a family."

He didn't laugh. He nodded. "I can't give you that by Saturday."

"I know. It won't be in the positions vacant section." She tried a smile, but it didn't work. Her mouth trembled instead. "No one can give me that."

Large and warm, his hand covered hers, offering comfort—or reassurance. She didn't know which.

"Some lucky man will."

"Where is he, then? He's had thirty-three years to find me." She focused on their hands to avoid the sympathy in his expression. What had possessed her to say that? She sounded like a self-pitying old maid whining, "Nobody loves me, nobody cares." He'd be nauseated. And all his defense systems would be sending out alarm messages in flashing red neon: *Desperate woman. Biological time bomb. Stay clear, stay clear.*

"Maybe he's not in Narooma."

Her spine stiffened, and with it, her tone. "Are you saying I should leave?"

"I'm not saying anything. But Narooma's not a big place. The world is."

"But you haven't found your soul mate out there in the big wide world."

He laughed—a scoffing little release of air—and relaxed against the back of his chair. "I'm not looking."

"Doesn't matter. When you meet her, that'll be that, whether you were looking or not."

He squeezed her fingers, then released his grip. "Spoken like a true romantic."

Brady refilled their glasses. Cutlery clinked on plates; knives scraped; crispy lettuce crunched as Phoebe helped herself to more.

"Do you have any qualifications?" he asked.

"An arts degree. Doesn't help much. It's not specific, and I didn't do honors."

"Looks good on a résumé."

"Makes me overqualified sometimes."

"Computer skills?"

"Reasonable. Plus bookkeeping. I did the accounts in the bookshop."

"Mmm. Shouldn't be hard to find you something. You're attractive, well presented, with good people skills and retail experience."

"I shall look forward to my new position."

Brady set his glass down. "Well, if I fail, you can come and work for me."

Phoebe laughed. It was a scoffing sound similar to his when she'd mentioned soul mates. "On your boat, Captain?"

"Sure. Why not?"

Chapter Four

In France?" Another gurgle of laughter bubbled to the surface.

"At the moment we are, but we're doing Greek Islands and Turkey next. Have you been there? It's fantastic." Brady's gray eyes bored into Phoebe's, sending his enthusiasm and passion directly to her brain. It would be fantastic. She'd love to travel and see all those exotic places—for a holiday, not an insecure, open-ended lifetime based on the casual suggestion of this guy.

Her expression must have implied she was seriously considering his ridiculous offer, because he said, "Do you speak another language? French? Greek?"

"Je parle français un peu."

"Très bon. Moi aussi." He grinned.

Phoebe stared at him. He was serious. Just because she could speak schoolgirl French, he expected her to pack up and join a yacht traveling aimlessly about the oceans of the world on the whim of people rich enough to charter such a vessel. He expected her to leave her house, her possessions, her friends, her life—everything she'd spent years painstakingly putting together from virtually nothing. Her place. Her home.

Brady leaned back in his chair, smiling a self-satisfied smile. "Perfect."

"No," she said loudly and firmly. "I don't want to do that. Apart from all the other millions of reasons, I get seasick."

He shrugged. "It was just a thought. We'll see how I go." The smile returned, infuriatingly smug.

Phoebe leaned her elbows on the table and glared at him. "You're enjoying this, aren't you? You're treating this as a game."

"Not a game. A challenge. I like a challenge."

"I don't. I've had enough of those, thank you. If I can't find a decent position, I don't know how I'll manage." A sick feeling settled in her stomach—dread. She couldn't bear the thought of losing her independence, renting out the house for income, moving, trying to squeeze her accumulation of treasures into a small, cheap unit or, worse still, having to beg for the use of a couch in a friend's place. Gavin or Phil and Ruth would gladly put her up for a week or so, but the humiliation would be unbearable.

"Don't worry."

Phoebe firmed her mouth and collected the empty plates. It was easy for him to say. He leaped to his feet.

"Leave those. I'll clear up. Would you like dessert? There's sinful ice cream in the freezer, and I'll make coffee."

She sighed. "Yes, please."

Extended sleep was elusive that night. Phoebe woke periodically and lay staring at the thin stripes of lighter darkness between the slats of the vertical blind. Brady's assurances of success had as much effect on her peace of mind as a single raindrop had on the levels in the Narooma water catchment.

And as for offering her a job on some luxury yacht . . . ! The whole thing was insane, completely and utterly insane. What did he expect she'd do? Scrub the decks? Make the beds? Be a glorified maid or a cleaner? No, thank you. It was all right for him; he was the captain. She'd be the lowliest member of the crew, the seasick one.

The night air was cloying and hot, the bedroom stuffy. She flung the sheet off her body and turned over. Was the window open? She got up, found the cord for the blind, and tugged. The two halves slid apart with a swish. The window was partly open. She slid the screen aside, pushed the window as high as it would go, and stuck out her head to drag in deep breaths of cooler night air.

"Can't sleep?" Brady's voice came from somewhere in the garden, lower, down the slope.

"Oh!" The word came out in a little shriek. "You scared me."

"Sorry." He moved closer, a dim shape in the moonlight, his pale shirt giving her eyes focus. "I can't go back to sleep." His voice was soft, intimate, floating on the warmth of the night.

"It's hot."

"Yes, but it's not that. I did sleep. I was really tired. Now I'm wide awake, and it's only four in the morning."

"Your internal clock is all upside down."

"That's why I prefer the sea. It's slower and you have time to adjust."

"Mmm." A yawn escaped.

"Sorry. I'll let you go back to bed." The dark figure melted into the shadows, leaving her with a curious sense of loss, disappointment that he hadn't asked why she was awake, hadn't suggested she join him in the moonlit garden.

Phoebe's eyes flickered open. Bright sunlight streamed in through the open blind; the sheet was tangled around her bare legs. She rubbed her face with both hands and groped for the bedside clock: 9:23. *Cripes!* The day was half over.

In the dining area, Brady was sitting at the table with the newspaper, a crumb-laden plate and a mug spread before him. He looked up and smiled. His gaze took in her shorts-clad legs and tank top and lingered on her body. Her heart lurched. How dare he be so attractive?

"Good morning. There's fresh coffee."

"Morning. Thanks, but I'll make tea."

He wore washed-out blue shorts and a loose, sleeveless, light gray T-shirt. His feet were bare. It was way too much exposed, muscled, tanned masculine body first thing in the morning: rounded biceps, with the tattoo—an anchor—clearly visible on his left arm, wide chest, flat stomach. A knowing smile slowly creased his cheeks. "Supposed to be ninety-five degrees," he said. "Good day for the beach."

"Aren't you forgetting something?" Phoebe wrenched her gaze from the areas of his torso under scrutiny and strode for the kitchen. She switched on the electric teakettle, then took yogurt from the fridge and began slicing a banana and strawberries into a bowl.

"No, I'm not. Apart from cleaning and waitressing, which you could get easily if you wanted to, there are several positions advertised, but I doubt whether you'd be interested in any of them."

"Like what?"

He turned a couple of pages and folded the paper open. "The golf course wants an apprentice greenkeeper."

"You're right. Next." She dumped the fruit peels into the bin labeled COMPOST.

"Someone wants a dog bather, but even though I know you'd jump at it, it's only a casual position."

"Very funny. Next."

"There's a position for a diesel mechanic and a welder with the local bus company."

"Next." She ground her teeth as she spooned yogurt over her fruit. He wasn't serious at all. He thought this was the biggest joke out there.

"Dental assistant."

"Wouldn't that need training? Surely they don't let just anyone loose in someone's mouth with that sucker thing?" She gave an involuntary shudder. It wasn't her favorite activity, visiting the dentist.

"Probably. It doesn't say. I'll call and find out. Maybe I should make an appointment while I'm at it. I haven't been to the dentist for years."

"You should look after your teeth. Bad things can happen otherwise." From his expression, she could tell he was as keen on dentists as she was. She jammed the lid back onto the yogurt tub and replaced it in the fridge. Maybe Brady was actively scared of the dentist. *Hah.* She said with a malicious little smile, "Someone I know developed an abscess in a tooth from not having regular checkups."

He scowled. "My teeth are fine. A photo shop needs an assistant."

Phoebe stifled her snicker. He was definitely scared. "Where's that?"

"Bligh's Photographics."

"Circle that one." She knew that place. It wouldn't be too bad.

"Already rang them, but the pay's rotten. They want a teenager. You can do better. This one might interest you . . . receptionist at a funeral home."

"What does that mean, it might interest me? Why?"

"Because it would be quite a good position. Difficult, though, I imagine."

"Is it Gray's Funeral Home?" She turned to see his expression, see if this was another joke at her expense, as she waited for the punch line.

He nodded without the glimmer of a smile.

"Ring them," she said as she dumped a tea bag in a mug.

"I have. They know you already. We have an interview at two this afternoon. Bring your résumé and references."

"Are you coming with me?"

"Of course. Moral support. I owe you that much." He held her gaze for a moment. "I didn't know celebrants did funerals as well."

"Yes. Sometimes. When the relatives don't want a religious ceremony. It's upsetting. I prefer weddings."

"I can imagine."

"There are a lot of retirees down here on the coast, so the funeral business is busier."

Phoebe poured hot water onto her tea bag and joined Brady at the table to eat her fruit and yogurt.

"Shall I phone the dentist?"

She nodded. He picked up his mobile phone, studied the paper, then dialed. Phoebe ate while he made the inquiries and agreed to an interview at nine in the morning. He was very smooth. No one would guess from his telephone manner what a rotten piece of work he really was.

"Thank you very much. Phoebe will be there at nine," he said into the phone before disconnecting. He tossed the mobile onto the table and sat back with a pleased grin, stretching his arms over his head. "Happy? Two interviews, two good-sounding positions. The dentist was very nice. Sounded keen to meet you, and it's on-the-job training. His name is Graeme Tucker. Know him?"

"No. I'll have to go home for my references." *Dental assistant? Why not?* Her lack of experience didn't appear to be a problem. Maybe she'd get cheap dental care.

"We can drop in on the way to the beach. I'd like to see your place."

She looked at him suspiciously, but he'd pushed his chair back and was on the way to the kitchen for a coffee refill.

"Did you go back to bed?" she asked.

"No. I did some washing and read, and when it was light, I walked down to those shops by the wharf and bought the paper. I called Alex."

"How is he?"

"Better. They're leaving in the morning. Be here about eleven, they think."

"Good." What a relief. Poor Lindy. Her meticulous planning hadn't made allowance for the flu. At least they'd have a couple of days to enjoy the company. And Phoebe wouldn't have to fight an overwhelming attraction to a man who was totally wrong for her. Totally wrong, full stop. Wrong for any woman.

"That was heartfelt."

"Of course. It's their party."

"Yes, but I'm quite enjoying the quiet with just us here. I told you I'm not into weddings."

Phoebe scraped up the last of her yogurt. "Well, that's the whole point of the exercise," she snapped. "That's why you're here."

As soon as Phoebe parked the Beetle in the white gravel parking lot beside Gray's Funeral Home, Brady knew this was wrong for her.

"No," he said.

"No what?" She pulled on the hand brake and turned off the engine.

"Don't go in."

"Why?" She turned to face him, eyebrows raised in astonishment. He hadn't seen her dressed up before, wearing makeup, hair held back with a comb. She wasn't simply a pretty girl; she was beautiful. When they'd dropped in at her little sky blue–painted house that morning, she'd picked up clothes suitable for an interview. And then she'd stunned him half an hour ago, when she appeared from her bedroom wearing a white summer blouse, a slim blue skirt, and high-heeled shoes. She looked elegant and sophisticated.

He couldn't let her work in a funeral home, not sweet, sensitive Phoebe. She'd be crushed under the weight of people's grief.

His mouth opened and closed; he dragged in a breath of hot air. It was easily ninety-five degrees already. "I don't want you to work there."

Phoebe gave a short, humorless laugh. "What you want hardly matters to me." She opened the door and slid one slim leg out.

Brady flung his door open and raced around to her side of the car.

He stood in front of her. "Please, don't. If the dentist bombs out, I'll find something else. I promise." She hesitated, and he saw the indecision in her eyes. A little frown creased her brow. The tip of her tongue moistened her lips.

"Uh, I don't know." She glanced at the solid polished-wood front door. "They're expecting me."

"I'll phone them and apologize."

"Why?"

"You should work somewhere that will make you happy. This won't. You'll be sad. It takes a special type of person to do this work."

Her frown deepened, and she made to step around him. He clutched her arm. "You're too . . . too . . ." He desperately searched for the right words to convince her. "You love marrying people, seeing them happy. Here you'll see people at their saddest."

"But I need a job, Brady." She was weakening. She didn't want to work here. The grief would overwhelm her, and she knew it. She was just anxious for the security of a pay packet.

"I'll take care of it. Don't worry." He stared into her eyes, willing her to believe him, wanting her to accept his offer, to trust him, to rely on him to take care of her, make right the wrong.

"I . . ." She shook her head almost imperceptibly and bit her lower lip, then shrugged.

He pulled his phone from his pocket.

"No," she said abruptly. "I'll have to go in and tell Mr. Gray myself."

He hesitated, the phone open in his hand.

"I have to explain to him personally. I live here; it's a small community," she added. She stepped aside and headed for the front door.

Brady watched her walk up the shallow steps with a determined tread and disappear inside. Would she ignore his plea and do the interview? He leaned against the car, but the hot metal seared his skin through his shorts, so he sat on the seat instead, with the door wide open and his feet on the gravel. He smiled. No, she wouldn't do the interview, because she'd left her manila folder with her references and résumé on the seat.

His tongue poked at that wretched tooth again. It had kept him awake the previous night. Maybe he should visit a dentist while he was ashore. Not the one Phoebe was seeing tomorrow, though. He wasn't admitting to her he had a toothache if he could possibly avoid it. She'd be so smug she'd be unbearable.

Another car pulled up nearby with the crunch of wheels on gravel. A woman got out. She straightened her skirt and, clutching her black leather handbag tightly in one hand, strode to the door with nary a glance his way. She had a folder under her arm. Not a bereaved person; another interviewee, for sure. She looked capable and strong, a much more suitable candidate for this position.

Five minutes later Phoebe came down the steps. She slipped her dark glasses on and walked slowly to the car. Brady rose as she approached.

"Any problems?"

"No. Mr. Gray was disappointed I withdrew my application." She opened her door and got in but didn't start the engine. Brady sat beside her in the bucket seat. He'd moved it back as far as it would go so he could stretch his legs out, but it still had a distinct sag in the middle. She turned to face him. "You were right. I couldn't work there."

The engine revved, and she reversed out of the space.

When they were on the road, he said, "I may have to go and sweet-talk Imelda after all." Good thing he'd prepared the way—secretly, before Phoebe woke up—by ordering flowers to be sent to the bookshop that morning with a note that said simply *Imelda, I was extremely rude yesterday. Please accept my apologies. Brady Winters.* "Maybe, but there's always the dentist, and thanks to those people in my house, I can last a week or so before it's desperate."

"I promised you'd be employed before I left," he said grimly.

A faint smile flitted across her lips. "Don't worry. I won't hold you to that. I was furious when I made you promise."

"You had every right to be." He sighed. She'd forgiven him already, was trying her best to reassure him. What an extraordinary girl she was. With any luck Graeme Tucker would recognize her special qualities and Brady wouldn't lose face. She didn't expect him to keep his word. That hurt almost as much as his tooth.

They drove in silence to the house. Inside, Phoebe headed for her room to change, and Brady headed for his to have a sleep. Wandering about the garden the night before had worn him out.

He paused at the top of the stairs to the lower level. "I'm taking you to dinner tonight, remember?"

She smiled over her shoulder. "Lovely. Thank you." But it wasn't her happy, wide smile. He'd effectively wiped that from her face the day before, when he'd ruined her peaceful life like the insensitive jerk he was.

"I'd better make a reservation. Is there somewhere special you'd like to go?"

She paused, her brow wrinkled in thought. "There's a new place connected to a winery a little way inland. Magpie's Nest. It's supposed to be good. Not cheap, though."

He shook his head. "It doesn't matter. We'll go there."

He opened the phone book and made the reservation; then he opened the Yellow Pages and looked up dentists. There were only two listings for Narooma, and he'd already talked to Doctor Tucker. He rang the other number. A recorded message said, "The surgery is closed until February fourth. For emergencies please call Doctor Graeme Tucker . . ." He didn't wait for the number. He already knew it. Was this an emergency? Not really. A pill would take the edge off the pain.

He went to his room, kicked off his sandals, and fell onto the bed, his mind filled with all sorts of alien thoughts and ideas, the main concept being, how could he make Phoebe smile again? How could he repair the damage he'd done? How could he make her like him? Trust him? For some inexplicable reason, he wanted her good opinion, and at the moment, he knew he was a long way from achieving it. When the others arrived the next day, the dynamics would change and he'd lose his chance in the reunion.

Tonight he'd have to impress her. Magpie's Nest had better not let him down.

His tooth hurt.

Phoebe spent the rest of the afternoon with a book under the shade of a large tree in the garden. After ten minutes, she gave up trying to concentrate on the intricacies of the plot and allowed her mind to wander—to Brady.

He wasn't quite what she'd originally thought, not as egocentric and selfish. He seemed genuinely concerned about her future now. It was rather late, unfortunately, but at least he was trying to put things right. And dinner at the winery would be a treat. A night out with a handsome man who was intent on appeasing her couldn't be all bad. She smiled. Not bad at all.

A dental assistant. That would never have occurred to her. Might be interesting. Certainly different from anything she'd done before. If Doctor Tucker liked her, she'd give it a shot. Why not? It was better than facing Imelda again. Even seeing Brady grovel wouldn't be worth having to do that.

Phoebe wore a white summer dress to dinner that night, the only dressy one she'd brought to the house apart from her pink celebrant's outfit. That week was supposed to be ultracasual—a week of having barbecues, spending lazy days at the beach, lolling in the garden, staying up late talking, catching up. She hadn't planned on job interviews and dining out. Going on a date—no, not a date. He owed her.

He wasn't thinking of it as a date. Brady was thinking of it as atonement.

She still needed to ask him questions about Alex. The Mexican-wedding story wouldn't go down too well at the ceremony. She needed other stuff. That night at dinner would be her only opportunity before the others arrived.

When he heard Phoebe's bedroom door close, Brady rose from the easy chair where he'd been waiting for her to join him. She appeared in the doorway, elegant in a white dress, shapely legs shown off to perfection by the short hemline and high-heeled sandals.

"You look beautiful."

She did. Stunningly beautiful. She'd done her hair differently, pulled it up in a soft updo, exposing her neck, tempting his fingers and lips. Thank goodness he'd packed a decent shirt and pants and wielded the iron that afternoon.

"Thanks. Shall we go?" She pulled car keys from her little clutch purse.

"We're going by taxi."

"Oh! That's not necessary."

"Yes, it is. You can't have a glass of wine if you drive."

"But it'll be so expensive, and I don't drink, anyway."

"Phoebe, it doesn't matter. Believe me."

She studied him with a slight frown clouding her face. "Are you sure? I don't mind driving."

"Positive. He should be here any minute."

"All right." But she was doubtful; the frown didn't leave her brow as she slipped the keys back into her bag.

He needed to kiss her, to reassure her. A friendly kiss, to apologize for the hurt he'd caused, to show he cared. She couldn't object. She hadn't before on the beach. The memory swamped him. A similar, overwhelming urge quickly become irresistible. He stepped forward and held her lightly by the bare shoulders. Her skin was warm under his fingers, her perfume intoxicating his already heightened senses. She turned her head, startled by the abrupt movement.

His lips landed on her partly opened mouth, and he felt her body tense with surprise under his hands. But then her shoulders relaxed, her mouth responded, and to his amazed delight she was kissing him. She was as tentative as he at first, giving light, gentle kisses, tasting, testing, then gaining confidence, increasing in passion and hunger. He didn't dare stop, in case she changed her mind; he didn't want to stop, couldn't stop. He pulled her close against him and slid his arms around her, feeling the curve of her waist and the swell of her hips. Exciting.

Her arms wrapped around his neck, her fingers twining in his hair. She groaned softly.

A car horn beeped twice outside.

Phoebe froze in his arms. "Taxi," she murmured.

"Let him wait," he growled. But she'd already extricated herself from his embrace and was hurrying from the room, leaving him frustrated, empty, and bereft.

Brady strode to the front door, smoothing his hair with shaking hands. He waved to the driver and turned inside to wait for Phoebe. What on earth had just happened? What would have happened if the taxi hadn't arrived? That wasn't what he'd planned at all. He didn't want to seduce her. He had, at first, when he saw her at the airport, but not now, when he knew her better. Now he had an obligation to her. She deserved better; she wasn't a plaything.

But she'd kissed him . . . so what did that mean? Had he completely misjudged her?

The whole thing was way too complicated. *Back off.*

Phoebe reapplied lipstick with a trembling hand. Her face was flushed, and her lips puffy and tingly from his kisses. *Good grief.* What a runaway train. So much for keeping a distance between them. How would they survive that night alone in the house with that memory roaming their minds? Would she have let it go further if the taxi hadn't interrupted?

She snapped the cap back on the tube and stowed it in her purse. Her hair was still in place, looked fine from the outside. Good thing no one could see the mess in her head. She drew a deep breath and walked out to meet him, stomach a tight ball of nerves. What would he say? If he apologized, she'd hit him. No one had ever kissed her like that. No one had ever had such an effect on her.

He smiled and held out his hand. The tension dissolved under the warmth in his eyes. She grinned.

"Fun, huh?" he murmured. He squeezed her fingers briefly and ushered her ahead of him to the waiting taxi.

Phoebe sat next to him in the rear seat. The road led inland through thick bush, and the sun, setting slowly over the hills, cast magical golden shafts of light between the trees. Brady stared out the window, hands clasped lightly in his lap. He had long fingers, tanned and wirily strong, the nails trimmed short. A faint scar ran across the knuckles of his left hand.

"How did you do that?" she asked, touching his hand lightly.

He looked down and spread his fingers wide so the pale line showed more clearly. "Got it caught in a line. Nearly took my hand off."

"Gosh. Must have been painful."

"It was." He cocked his head with a slight smile. "Hazard of the job."

"What would you have done if you had lost your hand?"

"But I didn't." He gave her an amused look.

She frowned. "But what would you do if you had an injury, or some sort of accident, an illness which meant you couldn't go to sea anymore?"

The smile faded. "I'd jump overboard." He stared out his window again.

Phoebe looked at the trees flashing past.

He picked up her hand and kissed the fingers softly. "My life is at sea, Phoebe. I'm not . . . I can't change that for . . . I won't change that for anyone . . . for you."

"I don't expect you to. It was just a kiss." Her voice came out calm and cool. He wouldn't believe her, but it was true. "I don't expect anything from you." She lowered her voice. "And don't expect anything from me based on that kiss."

He licked his lips. "I don't."

He held her skeptical gaze until she looked away. "I bet," she murmured.

"Put it this way," he said. "If there's anything on offer, I'll accept."

She gave a little snort of laughter. "You've had all there is."

"Fine." After a minute of silence, he said, "Can I have some more? Of the same?"

Phoebe laughed. "I don't think it's a very good idea, do you? Anyway, it'll be different when the others arrive tomorrow."

He sighed. "Sad but true."

"You'll get over it."

But would she? Sitting close beside him, hearing his voice, his laugh, the teasing; knowing the feel of his lips, the way his arms held her against his body, the incredible rush of desire and, most extraordinary of all, the overwhelming sense of the rightness she felt in his arms when in reality she knew he was totally wrong—all this was indelibly imprinted on her being.

"I need to ask you more questions about Alex," she said.

"Fine. Fire away." His relief at the change of subject was palpable.

Chapter Five

 S o what have you and Brady been up to here all alone for two days, Phoebe?" Alex asked when the expanded company sat around the table at lunch the next day. "I'm amazed you're still speaking to him. He's got a terrible reputation with women. Loves 'em and leaves 'em. Did he behave himself?"

He gazed at her with an attempt at solemnity, which failed due to his habitually cheery expression. She'd never seen Alex look glum, even now, when he was recovering from the flu and weaker and paler than usual.

"Of course," she retorted.

"I tried to misbehave," Brady said over the burst of laughter from bridesmaids Sophie and Kate and indignant huffing from Lindy. "She wouldn't have a bar of me."

He grinned at Phoebe, and she smiled with what she hoped was a demure expression. The happenings of the preceding two days would not be elaborated upon, they'd decided at dinner the previous night. Neither of them would tell Lindy about the Mexican marriage, but both would tackle Alex with the subject before Saturday. She wouldn't mention his part in her job disaster if he wouldn't mention their kisses. Not that she'd put it that way. "Don't expect any more," she'd said in the taxi, and he, with minor, obligatory protestations, had agreed—and kept his distance.

She held a professional position in this wedding, and she meant to maintain a certain level of dignity regardless of what the rest of the party got up to. Kate and Sophie were clearly here for a good time, whatever that might involve. Sitting on either side of Brady, laughing and flirting, they were exactly what a man with his approach to women would have had in mind that week, and with the unerring instincts of heat-seeking missiles, they'd latched on to him the minute they tumbled out of Alex's Magna. He didn't seem to mind one little bit.

What man would? Kate was vivacious and pretty and wore the shortest of shorts and the briefest of tops. Sophie, Lindy's auburn-haired best friend, five years older than Kate, had recently emerged from a relationship gone sour, so was, as she'd declared on arrival, "ready for some fun."

"My virtue's long gone," said Kate.

"I doubt I had any to start with," offered Sophie.

"Virtue is a highly overrated commodity," said Brady.

Phoebe picked at the salad on her plate, listening to the excited repartee punctuated by shrieks and yells of mirth. *Enough.* Brady was welcome to them and their games. He was here for less than a week. She'd had her turn, tasted temptation, and emerged shaken but with virtue intact. Far from being its own reward, virtue didn't offer much consolation to a heart under siege. Two days with Brady had shattered her placid existence, and she'd gone the range of emotions from stunned desire that first day, through astonished annoyance at his callousness regarding marriage and family, on to aghast fury, and all the way back to rampaging desire, fueled by his passionate kiss.

He'd displayed softer angles, but how glad she was now, as she observed the dynamic between him and the other girls, that she hadn't succumbed to that intense attraction, become another fleeting conquest, a holiday fling. But could she bear it if he transferred his attention to Kate or Sophie instead? Flirted? Kissed?

The conversation had veered to names while she wasn't paying attention.

"Do you, Phoebe?" Kate asked.

"Sorry. What?"

"Do you have to say both first names when you do the vows?"

"I usually do, yes."

"In case there's another Lindy Annabel and I'm marrying the wrong one," said Alex.

"You're such an idiot." Lindy leaned over and kissed him.

"What's your middle name, Brady?" Sophie asked.

"I don't have one."

"Dave's middle name is Rupert." Alex burst out laughing. "Brade and I cracked up at his wedding when the vicar said, 'Do you, David Rupert, take Angela . . .'"

"He hates it," said Brady. "What's your middle name, Phoebe?"

"I don't have one either."

"Mine's Marie," said Sophie. "After my French grandmother. Do you speak French, Brady?"

"Yes. And Italian and a bit of Greek."

"Wow. Say something in Italian. I love the sound of Italian. It's so sexy."

Brady fixed his eyes on hers. *"Non mi sente bene perche ho mal di dente,"* he said with slow, rolling intonation, a deep masculine tone, and a smile that promised heaps.

"Oooh." Sophie giggled and flapped both hands in front of her face.

Phoebe picked up her plate and glass, the cutlery rattling in her suddenly clumsy fingers. "Excuse me, everyone. I have to finish my notes for the service."

"We're going to the beach. Do you want to come?" asked Sophie.

Phoebe paused, forced a regret-filled smile. "No, thanks. I can't. I have to get this finished."

Brady watched her deposit her dishes in the dishwasher. She was nervous, tense—probably anxious to hear from the dentist about the job. He was too. It sounded good from what she'd told him after the interview that morning. She'd come out smiling and quite hopeful. "I think he liked me," she said. "He's seeing two other people this morning, and he'll let us know this afternoon."

He glanced at his watch. It was just after one, too early yet. If she landed it, they could relax and enjoy the rest of the week. He couldn't believe he cared so much.

"Are you coming, Brady?" Kate chirped as Phoebe headed for her room.

Brady turned to Alex. "How about you, mate? I'm just as happy to stay here and catch up." Especially as Phoebe wasn't going out.

Kate was cute but really full-on, and Sophie was downright dangerous. He'd seen that look before. She was the sort of woman who could rapidly become a liability, wounded and vulnerable with all her natural self-protective instincts shot to hell. Any man would do, and she didn't care about consequences until too late—a bit like himself. His old self. His pre-Phoebe self. How could he consider either or both of these girls with lovely Phoebe in the house and her kiss on his lips? He couldn't do it. What had happened to him? It must be the tooth, which had become a constant nagging ache.

"Maybe you should have a rest, darling." Lindy put a gentle hand on Alex's arm. She was a very uptight girl, handsome rather than pretty, with straight collar-length brown hair cut in a stern line and pale blue eyes assessing everything with disconcerting directness. Not a girl to be fooled with. She worked in a bank, Alex said. Refusing people's loan applications, probably.

"Yeah, I'm not over the flu yet. You girls go, and Brade and I'll stay here. We haven't seen each other for three years."

"We should see Mum and Dad, Kate," said Lindy. "I want to check the marquee and where the ceremony will be. I thought down by the pond, but it depends. Dad was talking about a flowering something-or-other which would make a nice backdrop—"

"After the beach," Kate cut in.

"All right. I can drop you and pick you up later. I have to check the caterers, the cake maker, and the florist this afternoon."

Kate rolled her eyes. "Calm down, Lindy. They'll manage without you breathing down their necks. You're here to enjoy yourself like the rest of us."

"And who's going to take care of all these last-minute details?" Lindy's voice rose several notches. Brady pursed his lips and edged his chair away from the table. This was exactly the type of scene he'd been dreading. Maybe he could sneak out without her noticing. His tooth was throbbing nonstop. He didn't want his head to join in.

"I'm sure they've all done weddings before, but if it's that crucial, can't Mum do some of it?"

"Mum has and so has Phoebe, but it's my wedding, and I need to make sure everything's perfect. I certainly don't expect you to do anything."

The sisters glared at each other. Any moment now, there'd be name-calling and hair pulling. It was time for the men to leave.

Brady stood up. "Excuse me."

Alex pushed his chair back with a loud scraping sound.

"Careful, darling." Lindy's furious gaze swung to him and then down to the floor, searching for scarring and scratches on the tiles.

"What?" Alex slumped in his seat and produced a feeble-sounding cough right on cue.

Lindy's mouth firmed. She shook her head. "Nothing. I'm sorry. . . . It's the stress."

He leaned over and kissed her. She rested her head on his shoulder for a moment while he murmured soothing somethings in her ear and caressed her bare arm.

Kate and Sophie made good their escape. They cleared the table, then went to change.

Alex said, "Do you have to do all that stuff today, sweetheart? You should rest too."

"I will when this is done. We brought your suit, Brady. Hope it fits." Lindy straightened and eyed him critically. "I had them alter it to exactly those measurements you sent." She rose. "I'll get it."

"It'll be fine," Brady said quickly. He added with cheerful enthusiasm, "Relax and enjoy yourself. It's a fantastic house. Phoebe and I have had a ball so far."

"Really?" Alex cocked a lascivious eye his way.

"We had a barbie the first night, went to the beach twice, lounged around, and last night we went to dinner at a winery she recommended. It was great." Why was he trying so hard to justify a platonic relationship? When he and Alex last met, he'd have played along with Alex's innuendo. The Brotherhood had standards.

"I'm glad." Lindy bestowed a smile upon him. A genuine one. Her others had had a tinge of disapproval lurking around the edge. He recognized that look too: that of the woman who mistrusts a man with no perceivable roots. It made him a bad prospect, and he never went out of his way to disabuse them of their opinion. Being a bad prospect was, generally speaking, a good thing.

"Phoebe is one of my oldest friends," she said as if warning him not to go there.

"She told me." He gave her a placating smile. "She's my friend too, now."

"Calm down, sweetheart," said Alex. "If Brady was going to ravish Phoebe, he would have done it by now. He never wasted any time when he spied a girl he liked."

"Don't be such a Neanderthal. Phoebe's not some cheap bimbo!"

"I know." Brady turned to Alex. "Cut it out, mate. You make me sound like a real jerk."

"You are." Alex stood up. "C'mon. Let's sit out there. Grab some beers on your way."

Lindy disappeared toward the master bedroom, presumably to unearth the suit she'd brought.

Brady deposited a beer in Alex's outstretched hand and plonked himself down next to him. He popped the top on his own bottle.

"Great to be back," he said.

"Yeah, it's been a while. Ever think of coming home permanently?"

Brady shook his head. "Nuh. Home is the *Lady Lydia*."

"Got it too good over there?"

"Yeah. When I stop enjoying myself, I'll think of something else to do. Hasn't happened yet."

"No woman on the scene."

"No way, mate."

Alex raised an eyebrow. "It's not that bad a deal. You just haven't found the right girl yet."

Brady laughed softly. "That's what Phoebe said." And he'd told her the right man might not be in Narooma. She had to look further afield, across the sea.

"What about Phoebe?"

"What *about* Phoebe?" Brady took a swig of his beer, deliberately avoiding catching Alex's eye.

"She's pretty."

"Yes."

"And nice."

"Yes."

"Did you get on all right?"

"Yes, of course. Why?"

Alex grinned. "She seemed a little tense at lunch. Thought you may have had something to do with it."

"So you make that crack about me trying it on with her? Good one, mate."

"All right. Not interested in Phoebe." Alex laughed. "Sophie's available."

No way was Brady commenting on either statement. "Phoebe's waiting on a call about a job."

"Phoebe has a job." Lindy appeared on the verandah with a gray suit over her arm. "She works in a secondhand book shop."

Brady put his beer on the table and stood up. "Not anymore."

"Really? She loved working there. I wonder why she left." Was he imagining that she sounded suspicious? Did she suspect he was involved? *Impossible*. Why would she?

"Is that my suit?"

"Yes. Could you try it on, please? If it needs altering, I'll take it with me this afternoon. The dress shirt is there too. "

"Thanks, Lindy." He took the suit and strode inside. Phoebe needed to be warned. Lindy the terrier was on the scent.

He tapped on her door.

"Come in."

"Hi." He stepped in and quickly shut the door. She was sitting cross-legged on the bed with her laptop open before her. Pretty and desirable. So innocently lovely. She melted him every time.

"Is that your suit?"

"Yes. Lindy wants me to try it on. Listen, she knows you're looking for another job, so if she asks, you'll have to tell her the truth."

Phoebe studied him. A little smile hovered on her luscious mouth. He mustn't focus on her lips, or he'd have to kiss her again—and neither of them wanted that. They'd agreed. He'd lied, but she hadn't. She'd made it very clear.

"She won't be very impressed by your behavior."

"I don't think Lindy's impressed by me full stop."

"But you don't care, do you?" She sounded surprised. Just what did Phoebe think of him that she would ask that question?

"She's Alex's bride. I don't want to upset her."

"Then I can't tell her the truth."

"I don't want you to lie on my behalf."

"Maybe it won't come up. She's rather preoccupied."

"With any luck." He grinned. "Heard from Tucker yet?"

"No."

"Okay. I'd better try this thing on." He draped the suit on the end of her bed.

"Here?"

"Why not?" He slipped the tailcoat off the hanger and shrugged it on. "Seems all right. What do you think?"

"Fine."

He dropped his shorts, ignoring her gasp of astonishment. "You've seen me in my swimmers; what's the problem?" He stepped into the pants and pulled them up. "Bit loose round the waist, but with a shirt they'll be fine. Yes?" He looked at her.

"Fine," she muttered. Her cheeks had turned a delightful shade of pink. *Sweet, sweet girl.* How he loved to tease her. She couldn't keep her eyes off his legs and tried so hard to pretend she wasn't looking.

"I'll go and model it for Lindy. Back in a sec."

Phoebe released a pent-up lungful of air. She stared at the blue shorts lying on the floor. He was incorrigible. But he had great legs. And he was right—she had seen him in his swimmers at the beach, and they were far more revealing than his jocks with a formal tailcoat and loose T-shirt hanging over the top. It wasn't the revealing of flesh that had surprised her; it was his act of changing in front of her and his assumption she wouldn't mind. She didn't.

But would he so casually do the same in front of Kate or Sophie? Maybe living in confined quarters on boats removed any inhibitions and, along with them, social mores. But he was the captain! Or so he said. What had he said to Sophie in Italian?

Five minutes later he was back, grinning. "Lindy's happy."

"Good."

He scooped up his shorts. "I'd better hang this suit up. How's it going? The service."

"Fine."

"Can I see?"

"No. What did you say to Sophie in Italian?"

He grinned but didn't answer. In the doorway he paused. "I made an appointment to see the dentist while you were doing your interview."

"Did you?" Phoebe kept her expression neutral.

"Thought I might as well while I was there. It's ages since I've been. I don't have a regular dentist. Too hard living on a yacht."

"Good idea. When for?"

"Friday at four-thirty. I was lucky, they had a cancellation."

He smiled and backed out, closing the door. He was definitely terrified. A smile spread slowly across her face. That oh-so-casual, offhand manner was a real giveaway. What a hoot it would be if she got the job and was allowed to grope about in his mouth while he was flat on his back in the dentist's chair. The grin turned into laughter, and she ended up collapsing backward onto her pillows with tears streaming down her face.

The barbecue was fired up again that evening, with Alex and Brady taking charge of the cooking in typical male fashion while the women ferried salads and crockery outdoors. Sophie and Kate hovered about Brady like a couple of bees round a dandelion.

Phoebe sat at one end of the wooden table and silently toasted herself in iced orange-and-mango juice. The dentist had called and offered her the job starting on Tuesday after the long weekend, with a day of observation whenever it suited her this week. He'd agreed to let her do it in separate shifts of a morning and an afternoon. The next morning and Friday afternoon would be ideal. Doctor Tucker seemed nice. Imelda wouldn't have been so flexible. Phoebe hadn't had a chance to tell Brady yet. She'd let him stew a little longer. And she wouldn't tell him about her Friday shift till he walked in and was safely strapped into the chair.

"Let's all go to the Tavern later," said Kate. "There's a band playing tonight. I feel like dancing."

"Great." Lindy walked over to Alex and slid her arm around his waist. "Feel up to it, darling?"

"Sure."

Brady caught Phoebe's eye. "I'm not big on dancing," he said. She made no comment. What did he expect? She liked dancing.

Sophie ran her hand down his arm. "But you'll come, won't you? You have to come, Brady."

"Everyone has to come," said Kate. "That's the whole point of this week. We party together."

"Fine by me." Phoebe avoided his attempt to hold her gaze by rearranging the plates. "Except I want a reasonably early night, because the dentist wants me to come in and observe tomorrow morning at eight."

"So you got it?" said Brady. There was no mistaking his relief, followed immediately by a smug grin. "Congratulations. I knew you would."

"Thanks." More like he *hoped* she would. "I'm glad you were so sure. I wasn't."

"But you're supposed to be on holiday!" cried Lindy. "Can't it wait till next week?"

"No, unfortunately. I need this job."

"But why did you leave the bookshop?"

Phoebe hesitated. It had always been hard to deflect Lindy when she wanted an answer.

"You love books, you said. You always have."

"The boss was getting rather difficult to work for," she said, but it didn't sound convincing.

"It was my fault," interrupted Brady. "I interfered and the old bat sacked her."

"What?" screeched Lindy while Alex said, "Whoa!" and the other two girls emitted delighted shrieks of horrified laughter.

"What did you do?" screamed Kate.

"I told her what I thought of her. She was abusing Phoebe, accused her of lying. . . ." He glanced at her. "Phoebe doesn't lie. I'd only just met her and I knew that."

"Good for you, mate!" Alex said, and slapped him on the back.

"That's all very well." Lindy rounded on Brady with indignant fury pulsing in waves from her body. "But she lost her job because of you. Did you think of that when you were being so protective?"

"No, but the woman totally overreacted. She's nuts. But it's worked out well. Phoebe has another job with a much nicer boss." To his credit, he kept his cool. Ship's captain in action.

"That's hardly the point, is it?"

Alex laid an arm round Lindy's shoulders and squeezed. "But, sweetheart, Phoebe's all right. She has another job."

Lindy pulled away with an irritated frown. "Well, I think it's incredibly irresponsible. How dare you interfere in Phoebe's life that way?"

"I know. You're right, and I apologized. Didn't I?" He turned to Phoebe with *help* written all over his face. This must be straining all his seams. She'd seen him in action with Imelda. Would he keep a lid on it with Lindy for Alex's sake?

"Yes," she said. "But I was furious with you too."

"Apologizing is the least you could do. I can't believe anyone would act in such an incredibly infantile way." Lindy glared. Phoebe knew that expression of old. She had the bone and was not letting go. "And what about apologizing to the poor woman you insulted?"

Phoebe raised her eyebrows and smiled innocently at Brady. "Good point."

Brady glanced from one to the other. Lindy was livid. Phoebe was enjoying herself at his expense. He couldn't blame her, but she'd let it go—or he thought she had. They'd made their peace, and she had a new job. Why couldn't Lindy accept that it wasn't her business? None of the others were carrying on like this. She was a real stirrer. What was Alex in for?

"She wasn't exactly rational." *Rather like you,* he thought but wisely refrained from uttering. His voice hardened. "No one should be spoken to the way she spoke to Phoebe. And anyway, Phoebe was thinking of quitting, weren't you?"

He wasn't going to curry favor with Lindy, or for that matter Phoebe, by admitting he'd sent the battle-ax flowers and a note of apology. If the women couldn't see his side of it, tough. And Phoebe was way better off, if everyone would only admit it.

"I was, but it doesn't make what you did right."

"Absolutely." Lindy turned to Alex. "See? Phoebe agrees with me."

"There are many ways to make a woman happy, but they're all wrong," said Alex. "Confucius said that."

"How right he was," muttered Brady, while the women huffed and puffed with indignation.

"We're outnumbered, mate," Alex said. "Wait till Dave gets here. Then we'll have a fighting chance. The Brotherhood reunited."

"I thought *we* were supposed to be together now, not you and your mates." Lindy flung her arms wide. "I thought you'd grown out of that silly brotherhood thing."

"Till death us do part," bellowed Brady, and he clinked his bottle against Alex's amid crows of laughter from Kate and Sophie. If that woman continued to carry on like a maniac, the Brotherhood would be going strong again in a very short time indeed.

Six people couldn't squeeze into Alex's car, so after dinner, Phoebe drove to the Tavern with Sophie in the back and Brady, wishing he didn't have to go, sitting beside Phoebe. After Lindy's tirade earlier, he wasn't game to upset her again by refusing to join in the group outing.

"I feel like dancing," Sophie announced, shouting over the engine noise into his ear from her seat behind him. "Promise me first dance, Brady?"

"If you insist," he said, shooting a glance at Phoebe. If he had to dance, he'd much rather do it with her. She was smiling, clearly looking forward to the evening and the ensuing few days of celebration. So was he, now that Alex was here and Dave was on his way. Dave was arriving late that night, apparently, instead of the next day. Phoebe's problem was sorted; she'd forgiven him; she was happy again. The only black spot was his aching tooth. The pain had spread to his jaw.

"This band is pretty good," Phoebe said. "They were on last week too."

"Great." Sophie started murdering "You Make Me Feel Like Dancing" in a bad impression of Leo Sayer. Or maybe she wasn't copying Leo; maybe her singing was just plain bad.

Phoebe joined in. Her voice was better. She flashed him a grin, and he rolled his eyes but had to smile. Her brown eyes sparkled, her face lit with happiness. She had the same carefree expression she'd worn when she picked him up at the airport—the one that had lasted about two hours after unadulterated exposure to him.

"Cheer up, Brady," cried Sophie when they finally ran out of words. "Don't be such a party pooper."

He touched his jaw briefly. "Sorry. My tooth's sore." *True.* The wretched thing was now an all-consuming agony.

"Oh, poor you. Toothache's got to be the worst. I had an abscess once. The pain was unbearable." Instant sympathy from Sophie, a sly little twitch of the lips from Phoebe.

"Good thing you made that appointment." She swung the Beetle into an off-street parking area, cruised down one row, paused while someone pulled out, then whipped smartly into the space. "Lucky." Another wide smile.

The place was packed, pulsating with rhythm from the band and the crush of people. The air conditioner wasn't coping, but nobody seemed to care. Alex and Brady fought their way to the bar for drinks while the girls waited as close to the open doors to the terrace as they could manage.

Sophie grabbed Kate's hand and yelled, "Let's dance." They moved away through the kaleidoscope of lights, bopping to the beat, and disappeared into the crush on the dance floor.

Lindy's brow was furrowed, and her gaze fixed on the area around the bar, where Alex had last been seen, in the dubious, dangerous company of Brady. Phoebe leaned in, put her mouth to Lindy's ear, and shouted over the deafening rendition of "Crocodile Rock." "Alex isn't going to change his mind."

Lindy's astonished face turned abruptly. "About what?"

"The wedding." Phoebe held Lindy's gaze until she bit her lip and looked away.

She nodded. "I know." A moment later she said, "But he's different around Brady. He's . . . I don't know . . ." She shrugged helplessly. "Maybe he's regretting being tied down. To me."

Phoebe shook her head. "He made his choice ages ago. He chose you over Brady and his mates."

"What if he thinks he made a mistake?"

"Has he said that?"

"No."

"Do you think you've made a mistake?"

"No!"

Her wide-eyed shock made Phoebe smile. "Lindy, relax and enjoy yourself."

"But Brady hates me."

"He doesn't. He's just grouchy because of his tooth." Why on earth was she making excuses for the man? His problem—one of them—was he was too used to giving orders and answering to no one except himself.

"Crocodile Rock" wound down, and in the relative quiet Lindy said, "Maybe he has an abscess. I guess that would hurt a lot. Poor guy." She screwed up her mouth in sympathy, then added, "Serves him right."

"Yes. My sentiments entirely." Phoebe nodded, straight-faced.

Lindy gave a little shriek of laughter. "Maybe he'll need a root canal. I hear that's horrible. Extractions. Dentures."

Phoebe's laughter bubbled to the surface. "And guess what? He doesn't know, but I'm going to be at the dentist's doing my training on Friday afternoon."

Lindy's face lit with unadulterated joy. "And Brady's appointment is . . ."

"Friday afternoon," Phoebe sang.

Brady edged carefully through the crowd, clearing the way for Alex, who held everyone's drinks on a tray.

"The girls are having fun," Brady said as they approached the pair of cackling women. The band launched into "Viva Las Vegas." Phoebe was right; they were good, but the lead singer looked more like a retired schoolteacher than Elvis.

Alex nodded. "It's great to see Lindy laughing. She's been really stressed lately. Phoebe's great company for her. Very laid-back and confident about the service."

"Mmm. Do you know her well?"

"Reasonably. We usually see her when we come down to visit Phil and Ruth." Alex served the drinks to Lindy and Phoebe. "Here you go, girls."

"Thanks." Two pairs of eyes flashed to Brady and away again.

"Having fun?" Alex kissed Lindy on the cheek. "You haven't laughed much lately, sweetheart."

"No, I know. I'm sorry for being a dragon, honey." She caught Phoebe's eye, and they both started up again with the laughing.

"What's the joke?" Brady looked from one giggling girl to the other.

Lindy stared round the packed room, jigging in time to the music. Phoebe poked at the ice in her drink with the straw. She suddenly gave him one of her brilliant, happy smiles. "Nothing. Girl stuff."

He was not touching that one. He did not want to know. "Dance with me?"

"Oh. Okay, thanks." She handed her glass to Lindy.

Bopping to Elvis took his mind marginally away from the tooth, at least enough to enjoy dancing with Phoebe, although anything too energetic jarred his jaw. When the song ended, she made no move to rejoin the others, so he stayed despite the crush and the heat generated by a hundred packed-in, gyrating bodies.

Two more tunes and he'd had enough. "I need a drink and some air," he said. Phoebe nodded, and he followed her to where Alex and Lindy were now perched on a couple of high stools against the wall.

"We're going outside for a breather," he said, reclaiming their drinks.

The terrace was wide and deep but also full of people, some polluting the fresh air with cigarette smoke. He followed Phoebe around the corner and down a couple of steps into a smaller, more secluded area with a barbecue and a couple of wooden tables and benches. The music wasn't as loud, but the air was clean and cool, with the familiar tang of sea salt.

He sat opposite her and slid her glass across the table.

"How's your tooth?" she asked.

"Painful." He took a long swallow of the now tepid liquid and grimaced.

"Rotten timing to happen this week of all weeks."

"Yeah, but I guess it serves me right for not having regular check-ups."

A quick grin slid across her face but morphed into a sympathetic smile. She leaned forward, suddenly serious.

"Brady, have you talked to Alex yet about the Mexican thing?"

"I haven't had much chance." And he'd forgotten all about it. Did it really matter? Why not leave things alone? Lindy was already delicately balanced on a tightrope of stretched nerves. Any extra little thing could set her off, and this was no little thing.

"I thought you might have mentioned it this afternoon when you two were out there on the verandah."

"I didn't."

She swallowed the dregs of her melted ice and lemon squash. "I suppose I'll have to, then."

"When?"

"The sooner, the better."

"Not now!"

She gave an exasperated shake of her head. "Of course not now. Tomorrow. You can mention it in the morning if you get a chance, because I'll be at the dentist."

Brady sighed. "Do you really think it's necessary? It's old news."

"Yes, it is necessary. And it's not old news to Lindy."

"But she's pretty freaked at the moment. This might really mess her up. Mess everything up."

"She should know. And before the wedding. If they love each other—which they do—it won't make any difference at all."

"I'll get us another drink." Brady swung his legs over the bench and rose. "I hope you're right, but I very much doubt it."

Her mouth was a firm line as she looked up at him, her brown eyes stern. "Then it will be on my head."

But it wasn't just her attractive head; it was his and Alex's as well. An enraged Lindy was not a pretty sight, and an enraged, heartbroken, shocked, and betrayed Lindy would register as a nuclear blast on the female-reaction scale.

Chapter Six

Wen Phoebe arrived at the communal house after her first shift with Graeme Tucker, it was deserted. She fished her phone from her bag as she headed for her bedroom and a change of clothes.

Lindy had texted.

At the beach. Lunch at O'Riley's. 12:30.

It was already one-thirty. Too late to go now. Phoebe sent a response. She stripped off her dentist-friendly pink blouse and floral-print skirt and pulled on a blue tank top and white shorts. She'd be given a uniform the next week: a fitted blouse with tiny yellow flowers on a sky blue background, white slacks. Neat. A reply came in.

OK. Visiting Mum later. Dad, A, D&B sailing this pm.

Phoebe sent back, *See you there.*

Dave and Angela must have arrived late. She hadn't heard them, and no one had been up when she'd left early that morning, but a new car was parked next to Alex's.

She would have a quiet afternoon. Lunch first. She could read the mail she'd collected from home after the dentist, finish the wedding service, then, later, drive over to visit Ruth with the girls and talk wedding talk until the men arrived for the rehearsal and dinner.

Munching a salad sandwich, she sat at the table studying her bank statement with a furrowed brow. The outlays were, as usual, getting bigger each month, but there was a satisfyingly large amount in the deposits column from the week's rental on her cottage. It was almost worthwhile to stay or even board with someone for the summer and rake in massive amounts of holiday rent. *Hmm.* People did it each year, she knew, but it always seemed an odd concept to move out of her own home and live elsewhere. There was something unwholesome about it, rather greedy.

A car engine sounded outside. A door slammed. The engine revved and faded. Phoebe half rose, expecting a knock, but the front door opened and closed. Someone walked in on confident feet.

Brady—with a face like a wet sock. He was a man in pain, and judging from all the signs, she knew he would not be a good patient. Typical male. Gavin with a cold was woeful.

"Hello. I thought you were sailing." She sat down and began bundling her scattered papers. When he looked that pitiful, she wanted to hug him, but he'd take any sort of consoling contact completely the wrong way.

He meandered into the living area and stopped. "I came home by taxi. They're still having lunch." He touched his cheek with tentative fingers and screwed up his face. "This tooth is too painful. I need a painkiller and to lie completely still. Plus my head's still pounding from that band last night."

"Didn't you enjoy yourself?"

"Yes, but I'm not used to loud music in a confined space."

"They say if your ears ring, your hearing is being damaged."

"Terrific. So I'll be deaf as well as having all my teeth pulled out." He walked across the room and carefully lowered himself to sprawl on the couch, all helpless legs and arms and woebegone face.

Phoebe snorted with laughter but hastily tried to cover it up, turning away with her little stack of letters.

"Go ahead and laugh," he said morosely.

"Sorry. But the dentist is really nice, and it's only one tooth, isn't it? He's not going to yank them all out." She clamped her mouth into a firm line to prevent the rising giggles. He had such a miserable expression. It must be painful, but really . . . "I'll get you a painkiller." If his crew could see him now . . . not to mention his megarich clients. "Gummy."

"Very funny. Thanks."

She went to the bathroom and found the pills. When she handed him a glass of water and the tablets, he said, "How did it go this morning?"

"Great. I really liked it. I know the receptionist, Felicity. She comes into the bookshop sometimes."

"Better boss than Imelda?"

She nodded. "Better pay too."

He swallowed and smirked over the rim of the glass. Phoebe had to smile back.

"Okay. You were right. Rotten methodology, but right."

"The end justifies the means." He rearranged his cushions and settled himself for a nap. "What are you doing this afternoon?" His eyes closed.

"Finishing the service, joining Lindy at her mum's. You are too. We're all having dinner there tonight and having a wedding rehearsal."

"Fine."

"Did you talk to Alex?"

"No."

Phoebe glared at his recumbent form. He wasn't even game to look her in the eye, and a toothache didn't prevent conversation. He had no excuse.

"Dave and Angela are here," he said with his eyes shut.

"Thought so. I saw their car." A surge of compassion rose suddenly. She moved closer and sat on one of the armchairs. "It's such a shame about your tooth. Spoiling your reunion and everything."

Brady opened one eye suspiciously. She perched on the edge of her chair, back straight like a good little schoolgirl, hands clasped in her lap. "Yeah, it's a bummer," he said. Was she genuinely concerned or was she secretly gloating? She sounded for real, and her expression was completely guileless. Phoebe was a sweetie; he was a cynic.

A little frown had appeared on her brow. She brushed a wisp of hair aside. She was so pretty. He knew her scent, the softness of her skin. "Doctor Tucker said you may need several appointments. He probably won't be able to do all the work on Friday, because there's not enough time, and he's booked up for the whole of next week."

"You mean I might have to stay on? Longer?" He sat up, shocked to the core. He hadn't expected that development. One visit was all he wanted. One visit was more than enough if the man knew his stuff—one short visit.

She nodded. "You might. Depends what's wrong. Unless you have a dentist you can see when you get back to wherever you're going . . ."

"I don't. I've avoided dentists. Anyway, I move around too much." A strangled groan escaped as his spine sagged onto the cushions. *Stay longer?* He'd have to change his flights, find somewhere to stay, get on to Michel to take over captain's duties, meet *Lady Lydia* later in Greece . . . What a nightmare. Maybe he should ignore the whole tooth thing . . . but that was what had caused the problem in the first place.

"I assisted at an extraction today." Her expression was all concern. "The patient said she didn't feel a thing."

He stared at her with his mind a total blank. She smiled tentatively and stood up. "Like a cup of tea?"

He shook his head numbly and closed his eyes against the whole horrible situation. Those painkillers were all but useless.

Phil's choice of spot was lovely. The parental house stood on a four-acre block surrounded by tall, elegant spotted gums, the straight pale gray trunks dotted with darker patches of peeling bark. In the center, the land sloped gently to a small ornamental lake covered with purple and white water lilies and fringed with tall green reeds. Flowering shrubs formed borders around stretches of lush grass, watered especially for the wedding, Phil informed them, by pumping from the lake. The service was to be held beside the water, with the lilies in the background and a gracefully arching Japanese maple providing shade.

Phoebe smiled at the assembled wedding party. "Okay, folks, here's what happens."

She outlined the mechanics of the service—where the groom and best men were to stand, who had charge of the rings, where Lindy was to appear from with Phil, where she would stand, where the bridesmaids would stand, the order of events. Everyone eventually took their places amid, as usual at these rehearsals, plenty of laughing and wisecracks.

"Like herding cats," said Phil, with a wink in Phoebe's direction. He grabbed his daughter by the arm and hauled her from the group to the house from whence she would make her entrance. Kate and Sophie followed.

Ruth and pregnant Angela sat sipping cold drinks on the verandah, watching the antics.

"When the music starts, you two start walking; then Lindy and Phil follow," Phoebe called. "Pretend music for now. Go."

Sophie and Kate started walking and singing, "Here comes the bride, fair, fat, and wide . . ."

"See how she wobbles from side to side," bellowed Dave.

"We don't know any more words," Kate said. "Keep walking, Sis."

Ruth and Angela joined in with Sophie and Dave, singing, "Dum dum de dah, dum dum de dah," until Phil and Lindy arrived laughing before Phoebe.

"Perfect," she said.

She continued with a rundown of the service—the vows, the ring, the special reading by Sophie of Lindy's favorite poem, the signing—ignoring the silly running commentary by Sophie, Kate, and Dave. She'd heard all the excited chatter before. It was part of the fun of weddings. It was a pity Brady wasn't up to much. In such obvious agony, he was severely handicapped. He stood with a smile frozen in place and did his bit with the rings on autopilot.

He should be fine for the service, though. Doctor Tucker had assured her he would alleviate the pain and deal with the major problem on Friday. Not that she was telling Brady that. It might be petty, but it was a satisfying private compensation for the ordeal he'd put her through so cavalierly when he insulted Imelda.

Alex's second best man, Dave, was a loud, jovial bear. He had dark hair and beard, round face, round body, hairy legs emerging from shorts, beer in hand. He was the joker of the pack. The trio had slipped immediately into familiar mode, with verbal shortcuts and in-jokes flying. The Brotherhood was reunited.

Lindy wasn't amused, but Alex held her hand firmly, which was reassuring and smart on his part. He must know how insecure she was feeling at the moment.

"Do you say the thing about anyone objecting?" asked Kate. "I've never been at a wedding when anyone objected. Have you? That'd be hilarious."

"No, never." Phoebe smiled at Lindy. Hilarious? What was Kate thinking? But she'd always enjoyed baiting her serious big sister.

"Don't be ridiculous. Why would anyone object?" Lindy demanded. "Trust you to bring up something like that."

"I'm just asking Phoebe," Kate huffed indignantly. "I didn't mean anyone would."

"No one's going to object, Lindylou," said Phil. "Katie's teasing. Behave yourself." He gave Kate a strict, well-practiced fatherly frown.

"I'm not teasing, I'm interested. That's all. Sheesh!"

Phoebe caught Alex's eye. He smiled the smile of an innocent. Had Brady spoken to him? She'd guarantee not. She'd have to catch him herself, as soon as possible; she couldn't let it go any longer.

"Of course, there could be one person who would object, d'you reckon, Brade?" Dave hummed the opening phrase of "South of the Border" and burst into a raucous laugh.

"Who?" Lindy's rise in pitch was enough to shut up the most insensitive of clods. Her panicky eyes swung from Dave to Alex, skated over Brady, and landed once more on Dave. Alex's smile wilted.

Phoebe's mouth felt as though the dentist's spit sucker had been in action; her stomach tightened. She glanced at Brady. His face had the Botox look. "I doubt it very much," he said through almost clenched teeth.

"Of course no one will object," Alex said confidently, then gestured to Phoebe. "What's next?"

"Just a minute!" Lindy said. "What did you mean, Dave?"

Dave's eyes flicked from Alex to Lindy and finally the penny clanged into place. "Nothing. Just kidding, Lindy. Being stupid. Sorry."

That wasn't good enough. He didn't even convince Phoebe, and she wanted to be convinced. Phil was frowning, a half smile clicking on and off, but Lindy had the scent, hot and strong in her nostrils.

"What's that tune you sang?"

" 'South of the border, down Mexico way,' " said Phil. "What does that mean?"

"Private joke," muttered Dave. "It was something that happened when we were in Mexico years ago, not important." The exposed bits of his face now resembled a very ripe tomato.

"Why can't you tell us?" asked Sophie.

"What's the big secret?" Kate said with an expectant grin.

Phoebe raised her voice over the gathering storm. "Listen, can we finish the rehearsal, please?"

"Yes, let's." Alex sent her a grateful smile and squeezed Lindy's hand.

"So after you've all signed, I sign. While that's happening, your guitarist is playing some music—correct, Lindy?"

"Yes. He's playing 'A Whole New World.'" Her mouth quivered.

Dave needed gagging—and maybe a bag over his head for good measure.

"Lovely. Then I'll present you to the guests and that's it. Apart from the photos and the party. Thanks, everyone."

"Thank you." Lindy stepped forward and wrapped her arms around Phoebe.

Phoebe returned the hug. "It'll be beautiful, Lindy. Don't worry."

Alex kissed her cheek. "Thanks."

"I need to talk to you."

"Why?" Lindy's eyes narrowed, skipped from Phoebe to Alex.

Phoebe smiled. "Secrets. I just need a couple more things for my part in the service. Now, Alex?"

"Fine."

"Can I come?" called Brady as Phoebe and Alex began walking away round the lake toward the rear of the property.

"No." Phoebe sent him what she hoped was a glare. "You've had your turn." And he had failed dismally. *Hopeless.*

When they were out of earshot, Alex said, "What do you need to know?"

"I need to know why you didn't mention to me, or presumably Lindy, that you married a girl called Juanita in Mexico."

His mouth dropped open; he gasped but recovered. "But that was years ago. I'd forgotten all about it!"

"Obviously Brady and Dave haven't."

"Brady told you." He gritted his teeth. There were cracks in the fabric of the Brotherhood.

"Yes. He thought it was a joke. Like you. It isn't." She sucked in a breath and exhaled. *Men!* "How are you going to explain it to Lindy? Those two are bound to let it slip one day. Dave already nearly did. The longer it goes, the harder it'll be and the less you'll be able to make Lindy understand why you kept it secret."

"I didn't keep it secret. I didn't even think of it. I haven't thought of it for years!"

"Don't you think the fact you married someone else matters?"

He screwed his face into a perplexed grimace. "Why couldn't Brady keep his mouth shut?"

"That's hardly the point. Why should he?"

"But it's not . . . It wasn't . . ." He stopped and faced her with an expression of real fear. "It won't affect our wedding, will it? Legally? Am I a bigamist?"

"No, not legally. Morally is another matter."

"Morally? It was years ago. Everyone's forgotten all about it. Anyway, lots of people get married for the second time."

"But you should have told me. You need to be honest. With Lindy of all people. You know what she's like; she'll keep digging until she finds out."

"She'll be very upset." *Understatement of the year.*

"Not as upset as if she finds out after the wedding. Anyway, give her some credit. It might not worry her at all. She loves you, remember?"

"Not worry her? Ohhh." He paced, thumping his fist into his open palm. "What will I do?"

"Tell her."

"Now?"

"Wait here and I'll send her over."

Alex stared at her for a moment, looking like a trapped rabbit. He swallowed, nodded.

Phoebe turned and strode back to the house. Lindy had joined Ruth and Angela on the verandah to sip chilled drinks. Phoebe climbed the steps to join them.

"Alex wants to see you, Lindy."

Lindy sprang to her feet. "Okay. Thanks for the rehearsal, Phoebe.

I'm feeling much happier now. Everything's falling into place beautifully."

"It'll be lovely, darling." Ruth stretched out a hand and patted her daughter's arm as she passed.

Phoebe opened the sliding door and entered the house in search of Brady. He needed to be on hand for the fallout. So did Dave. Her insides churned. Was telling Lindy the right thing to do, or was Brady right? Were the men right? Was ignorance bliss? Lindy was certainly blissful. Now Phoebe didn't know.

Brady was in the kitchen with Dave, raiding the fridge for cold beers.

"Not having one, mate?" Dave thrust a bottle at Brady.

"No. The cold really hurts the tooth, and anyway, I'm taking painkillers. Not a good mix."

"Never would have bothered you in the old days. Must be going soft in your old age."

"Yeah. Something like that." Brady met Phoebe's gaze with a raised eyebrow.

"Drink, Phoebe?" asked Dave.

"Juice, thanks."

She took the glass he handed her. "Alex is telling Lindy about Juanita."

Dave nearly dropped his beer. "Now?"

"Why, Phoebe?" demanded Brady.

"Because I insisted."

He shook his head. "You're wrong. Totally and utterly wrong! You know what'll happen? She'll freak out and cancel the wedding."

"She won't."

"She will. She's the most uptight bride I've ever seen." Dave grimaced and swigged down half his beer. "Ange wouldn't care—lots of girls wouldn't care—but Lindy . . . phew."

"I hope you're prepared," said Brady.

Phoebe bit her lip. Was she prepared? "It's the right thing to do, and he should have done it ages ago," she insisted. "To be moral he should tell her."

"Right isn't necessarily best."

"Or smart," added Dave. He flung his arms wide. Liquid slopped from the bottle onto the floor. "For heaven's sake, we were twenty, drunk, and stupid."

"It's not the marriage thing; it's the honesty, the trust," Brady said, with more perception than she'd given him credit for. "Isn't it, Phoebe?"

She nodded. And it was about the sanctity of marriage, the preciousness of those vows. Tears pricked her lids. Brady understood the honesty angle, but he'd never understand the beauty of the marriage vows, the completeness of promising to love and care for that one person forever, the security it implied. It was a major step that should be taken with all one's heart and soul—not flippantly, not drunkenly, not as a joke one night in a foreign country because it seemed like a good idea at the time, a funny anecdote to share with the guys.

"I'd better see what's happening out there," she muttered, and fled before she cried in front of them, those two unromantic Neanderthals staring at her as if she was from another planet. How had Angela ever fallen for Dave? How could Phoebe contemplate falling for Brady?

What?

Never.

Ruth was halfway down the steps when Phoebe reached the verandah. Angela sat straight, baby belly bulging, her attention fixed on the two figures on the far side of the lake. One was running with hands clasped to her face; the other stood for a moment, arms hanging helplessly by his sides, then walked slowly away toward the trees.

"Oh." Phoebe's fingers flew to her lips.

"What's happened?" Angela's voice choked on a sob. "They were walking along together, and then suddenly Lindy started crying. She pushed Alex away. What's wrong?"

"Alex needed to tell her something." Phoebe started down the steps after Ruth, who was now hurrying to intercept Lindy.

"Tell her what?" cried Angela.

The sliding door scraped open, but Phoebe didn't turn. She knew who would be there. Brady and Dave could deal with their mate.

Lindy was the one in need of support. When Phoebe reached the two women, Lindy was sobbing in her mother's arms. Ruth's bewildered face turned to Phoebe, then back to Lindy.

"What's happened, darling?" she said. "Tell me."

But Lindy was crying too hard to speak.

Phoebe licked her lips. "Years ago when the guys were in Mexico, Alex married a Mexican girl. It wasn't a legal ceremony, but it was a marriage. . . ."

"You knew?" Lindy, betrayed on all sides, lifted a tear-sodden face from her mother's shoulder. "You knew and you didn't tell me?"

"Didn't tell you what?" Kate and Sophie arrived breathless, eyes shining, faces eager for information. Angela lumbered close behind.

"Alex is already married." The words barely emerged between heaving sobs.

"Married?" shrieked Sophie. "Oh my goodness! The utter rotter."

"He's not married," Phoebe insisted over the screeches and gasps. "It wasn't a legal ceremony."

"Why did he tell you two days before the wedding?" demanded Kate, bristling with sisterly indignation.

"I don't know." Lindy's swollen eyes swung to Phoebe. "Do you? You seem to know all about it." She'd straightened from Ruth's embrace, regained control, homing in on Phoebe as the troublemaker.

"I only just found out. Brady told me, and I told Alex to tell you." It didn't seem such a good idea now. It seemed a terrible idea, the worst ever. "I thought it was important he be honest. I'm sorry."

"Is that *your* decision to make?" Lindy pulled away from Ruth's restraining hand. "You must have known I'd be upset. How could you insist he do something like that? Don't you want us to be married?"

"Of course I do," Phoebe yelled. "He wants you to be married too."

"It won't affect the wedding at all, darling," said Ruth in her most soothing voice. "Why should it? Alex chose you. He loves you."

"He chose her first."

"I told you: I was drunk and I was about twenty years old. It meant nothing."

Sophie and Kate shrank back a pace as Alex stepped forward,

hand outstretched, face a distraught mess. Brady and Dave stood on either side of him, clearly wishing they were anywhere but there.

Lindy's spine stiffened. She raised her head to a most imperious angle. Gone was the wilted, sobbing girl. "And will our marriage mean as little to you? Will our vows mean nothing?"

"Sweetheart . . ."

She ignored his hand and his plea, his desperation. "It's not the girl. I understand that, Alex. It's the principle. I never considered marrying anyone until I met you. I had other boyfriends, of course, but no way would I have married any of them for fun. Or because I was drunk. Marriage means much more to me than that. *Our* marriage did, our vows, our promises." The facade collapsed; tears returned in a flood. "I thought I knew who you were. Now I don't think I do."

Ruth's comforting arms surrounded her again.

Alex's voice came hoarse and broken into the shocked silence. "Don't you want to marry me anymore, sweetheart?"

Lindy's reply, buried in Ruth's shoulder, was almost inaudible. "I don't know."

Then Kate and Sophie closed in, and Lindy was hustled away to the safety of the house.

Alex turned, his face twisted in pain and grief. "Is that what you wanted, Phoebe? Are you happy now?"

He strode away, cursing. Dave stood, irresolute, wordless and jokeless for once, then headed for the verandah hand in hand with bewildered Angela, her free palm pressed against her bulge.

Phoebe's legs gave out, and she slumped to the grass, tears hovering, then spilling. Brady stood over her, an ominous dark shadow. He drew in a deep breath, exhaled fiercely.

"Say it," she whispered.

"I don't need to." His voice chilled her to the core.

Chapter Seven

Brady spun about and strode away. Phoebe was such an infuriating innocent. The world wasn't black and white, the way she wanted it to be. People were confused, confusing, and complicated, and they did peculiar, inexplicable things that couldn't be made right by a few words. Sometimes things were better left alone, unspoken, put away in dark cupboards, and forgotten. There they would do no harm.

Weddings and women—what a disastrous combination.

He came across Phil, firing up the barbecue, at the rear of the house.

Phil glanced up. "Thought I'd get this started. You chaps must be starving by now. The girls do natter on with all this wedding stuff. Be glad when it's over, between you and me." He cocked an eyebrow at Brady. "You too, I'm guessing? Anxious to get back to the sea?"

Phil didn't know! He'd missed the explosion.

"Umm. There's been a bit of a glitch, Phil. . . . Lindy and Alex . . . Lindy's very upset . . . in tears, actually." An image of *Lady Lydia* flashed before his eyes. Serene and lovely, cutting through the blue water, sails full, gloriously uncomplicated, keen and willing, silent. The perfect female.

Phil laid down the grill scraper. "In tears? Why?"

"Alex told her about something that happened years ago—maybe twelve or even fifteen . . . in Mexico." There were a few more wrinkles on Phil's brow now; he was surprised, uncomprehending. Brady stumbled on. "Alex got married to a girl there. The whole thing lasted a day or so. It was stupid and meant nothing—and it wasn't legally binding, but . . ."

"Why on earth did he tell her now? Why tell her at all?"

Indeed. Brady hesitated. Phil would find out soon enough, and Phoebe *was* the great advocate of honesty. . . . "Phoebe insisted on it."

"How did she know? Who told her?" No avoiding this question either. Phil's clear blue eyes had him pinned.

"I did. I shouldn't have."

"No, you shouldn't have. Not Phoebe."

"She was asking about Alex for the service. You know, anecdotes . . . I didn't know her very well—don't know her very well. I was being flippant, joking, but she went crazy. She said as celebrant it put her in an awkward position."

"She's one of life's innocents. We love her dearly, but she sees the world through rose-colored spectacles." Phil rubbed a hand across his jaw. "How's Lindy taking it?"

"Crying. Angry. More at the fact that Alex hadn't told her before than the fact that he'd married someone . . . although she did say something along the lines of 'would he treat their wedding vows the same way.' "

"Hooley dooley, what a mess. I think I'd better keep away from the women and talk to Alex."

"Actually . . . would you talk to Phoebe first, Phil? She's pretty upset too."

"Shouldn't you? You put her in this position."

Talk to Phoebe? Again? Brady shook his head. "She knows you better." He added with a tight little smile, "And I'm too annoyed with her. I warned her over and over not to bring it up."

Phil gave him an odd, searching glance, then smiled. "All right."

"She's by the lake. I've no idea where Alex is."

Phil headed for the corner of the house, striding past the lushly populated herb garden he'd proudly shown them earlier. Thank goodness he was a calm, even-tempered man, used to his women and their hysterics, no doubt. Brady slid the back door open carefully and crept in, ready to retreat in haste if necessary, ears on alert for female wails. The murmur of voices came from the bedroom end of the house. The kitchen and living area were deserted. *Phew. Safe.* He walked across and peered cautiously through the fly screen toward the lake. Dave and Angela were still on the verandah, sitting close together, murmuring, heads inclined toward each other. Oblivious to his presence.

Phoebe sat on the grass where he'd left her, a small figure, forlorn and alone. The evening light cast a purple and gold tinge over the scene. The tinkle of bellbirds rang from the treetops. So beautiful for such a fraught situation. Phil appeared, sauntering along in his khaki shorts and white golf shirt, bald patch among the gray fringe clearly visible from Brady's elevated angle. He paused next to her for a moment. They were too far away for Brady to hear anything. The pale oval of her face turned Phil's way. Phil sat down, legs bent, hands resting on his knees. Phoebe's hand brushed across her face. Was she crying?

Brady's stomach tightened at the thought. His fingers clenched and straightened. He ran his tongue over his lips. Phil was with her. He'd say the right things, fatherly things to comfort her—better things than Brady could manage.

If he went outside to join Dave and Angela, she'd think he was spying. He wasn't. He was . . . What was he? Interested, concerned, perhaps? He might be angry, but he didn't want her soul destroyed. She'd acted from a pure motive, wrong though it might have been. But many great wrongs were done out of pure motivations, in the name of a greater good.

He'd acted the same way in the bookshop, completely spontaneously, convinced he was right. His pure motive, saving Phoebe from an exploitative, unpleasant, rude boss, had resulted in a positive outcome—eventually. Phoebe had a better job with better pay and a good boss. Was that pure luck?

Would this situation resolve itself in an ultimately positive way? Was Phoebe right? She thought she was, and she stuck to her position. If those two loved each other, they'd survive this bump. If they didn't handle it successfully, they were better off unmarried. They both could agree on that.

His tooth ached.

He flopped into the nearest armchair. Where was Alex? He hadn't taken the car, which was good. Safer, at least. He must be walking it off.

A few minutes later Sophie appeared in the doorway and headed for the kitchen, face grim. She flung open the fridge.

"What's happening?" He sat up. "How's Lindy?"

"Angry. Upset. What do you expect?" Her glance was scathing in the moment she granted him her attention.

Brady grimaced and subsided silently into the chair. She was the wrong person to ask. Sophie was the woman recently wronged by a man. Brady was a man; therefore, he was one of the Evil Ones. Cupboard doors opened and closed as she loaded up with whatever sustenance she'd sought; then her footsteps receded toward the Women's Lair.

Surely Ruth would talk some sense into her daughter, make her see that the whole thing was an overreaction. He closed his eyes. That wretched tooth throbbed unmercifully now, all the time. Friday couldn't come fast enough. Hard to believe he actually looked forward to visiting the dentist.

Voices sounded outside on the verandah. Phoebe and Phil were talking to Dave. Angela said something, the door opened, and they all trooped in.

"Time to eat," said Phil. "I'll see what's happening." He strode down the corridor to the bedrooms.

"Phil thinks this is crazy," said Angela. "So do I." She kissed Dave's cheek. "If you'd told me that you'd married someone else, I would've been glad you came to your senses, left her, and married me."

"You're one in a million." Dave returned the kiss.

Fingers clasped, eyes reddened, Phoebe said nothing for a change. She'd said more than enough.

"I agree, Angela." Brady sighed. "Better not to have said anything, though, knowing Lindy."

"But you don't know Lindy, do you?" snapped Phoebe suddenly. Her eyes flashed fire at him. Why was she mad at him? He'd tried to avoid exactly this situation.

"I knew she'd react like this. You didn't, and she's supposed to be your friend!"

"That's not the point, and given your attitude towards marriage, I wouldn't be surprised if you were secretly pleased the whole thing might be off."

"I'm not!" cried Brady above the clamor of Dave's "Hey, that's a bit rough," and Angela's "I don't think that's fair, Phoebe."

She ignored the indignation. "I can see why Lindy feels she's being ganged up on. You two joining forces with Alex as soon as you get together . . ." Obviously she meant that remark for him rather than Dave; her glare could shrivel a weaker man's ego to a crisp. This was a new and surprisingly aggressive Phoebe. She was far tougher under those tears than he'd imagined. Right or wrong, she had the courage of her convictions; he'd give her that.

"That's not true!"

"I never felt that," Angela said mildly.

Phoebe switched her attention, modifying her tone. "That's because you're a different type of person."

"Meaning?"

"You're more easygoing, less demanding."

Angela's eyebrows shot skyward. "Am I? Is that a compliment?"

"Yes," said Dave hastily. "Let's get this dinner under way."

"Good idea. Come on, Phoebe." Angela headed for the kitchen. "Where's Alex?"

Brady glanced at Dave, and they exchanged shrugs.

"Go and find him and bring him back. Those two have to sort this out."

"Okay, love. C'mon, mate."

Brady followed Dave out the door with a heartfelt release of air. Somehow Phoebe had managed to imply that this mess was basically his fault. How had she done that?

Phoebe and Angela ferried cutlery and plates to the long dining table.

"Don't worry, Phoebe. It'll work out. If they can't get through this, they shouldn't be married."

Phoebe thumped knives and forks into place. "That's what I think. The guys don't, though."

"Dave does. I don't know about Brady."

"I don't know about Brady either."

"He's very good-looking." Angela's eyes crinkled as she smiled. She turned away to fetch the salt and pepper shakers from the bench. "Don't you think?"

"Yes, but his personality could do with a makeover." Thank goodness Angela's back was turned, or she'd be treated to a display of overripe-strawberry-faced embarrassment. That was the main problem with Brady: he was completely and utterly physically attractive and continued to be so regardless of what objectionable words came from his mouth. The only antidote to that attraction was focusing on the obnoxious aspects of his character until he left Narooma. And there were plenty of those to focus on.

"You were a bit hard on him, though, don't you think? He's never given any sign to Dave or me that he didn't think we should get married. And I don't think he feels that way about Alex and Lindy either. He seems very happy for us all." Angela's mild tone masked the chastisement. She plonked the pepper shaker on the table and patted her tummy. "Ooh, Bub's kicking."

Phoebe's face grew even hotter. "It's not anyone in particular; it's the whole deal. He's anti-marriage on principle."

Angela tilted her head, considering. "That's all right. He doesn't have to get married."

She'd missed the point entirely, but now Phoebe wasn't sure what the point was or had been. Whatever it had been, it had exploded in her face, causing widespread collateral damage.

Lindy emerged from the bedroom with the others trailing behind her. She walked zombielike past Phoebe, slid the screen door open, and sat on the verandah, staring into the tree-obscured distance. Phil escaped to tend the barbecue. Ruth took a plastic-covered platter of meat from the fridge and joined him. Kate and Sophie began putting together a salad. No one said a word.

Angela murmured, "Excuse me," and headed for the bathroom, leaving Phoebe standing by the table. Phoebe joined Phil and Ruth outside rather than endure the frigid waves emanating from the would-be bridesmaids.

"I'm sorry."

Ruth sent her a tight little smile. "Heaven knows what we'll do if they don't sort this out. How on earth will we tell all the guests not to come? Alex's parents and grandparents are en route already. Mum and Pop are arriving in the morning, and Phil's mother's flying in from Newcastle in the afternoon. They're all staying on afterwards too, so we'll have the house full for a fortnight. It'll be an absolute nightmare if the wedding's canceled." She picked up a scraper and poked at the grill aimlessly, put it down again. "I can just hear my mother now. We'll never hear the end of it. It'll be all *her* humiliation and *her* embarrassment."

"It's well on the way to being a nightmare even if the wedding's not canceled, with that lot staying here. Ruth and I were planning on running away." Phil winked at Phoebe. "Cheer up, love. That face would depress the Dalai Lama. It'll be all right."

"But it's all my fault." She bit hard on her lip to stop its trembling. "If you have to cancel everything . . ." The concept was unbearable, impossible to imagine. Her fault. Her and her insistence on honesty.

"Best to get these things out in the open. We'll all be laughing about it in a year's time." He didn't look totally convinced, despite the confident tone.

"Where are the boys?" asked Ruth.

"Gone to find Alex."

"He won't do anything silly, will he?" She flashed an anxious glance at Phil.

"Doubt it. He was on foot; he can't go far." He flipped a steak. "If they don't turn up soon, they'll miss dinner."

"Should I talk to Lindy?" Phoebe asked.

"Leave her be for now," suggested Ruth.

"She's not seriously thinking of canceling, is she?"

"I hope not." Phil stabbed a sausage, and fat leaped out and sizzled on the hot plate. "Sophie's not helping much," he added. "Going on about how men can't be trusted. She even gave *me* a funny look."

"You?" Phoebe would have laughed if she hadn't been so close to hiding under a rock. Phil was devoted to his wife, and everyone knew it within five minutes of meeting them.

"She did not," said Ruth. "She's had a rough time lately, that's all."

"Well, she's not helping our Lindylou by lumping poor Alex in with her no-good exes. He's a decent bloke, and I like him a lot."

"So do I," said Ruth. "So do I. Should we call Esther and Joe?"

"No point alarming them unnecessarily, and anyway, Alex should talk to them if it comes to that. They're his parents."

Phoebe closed her eyes. It got worse and worse. Every second brought a new ramification to the disaster.

"Here they come." Ruth's delighted cry made Phoebe's eyes pop open. The three men rounded the corner of the house.

Flanked by Brady and Dave, Alex walked straight up to Phil and said, "I'm really sorry this happened, Phil. And Ruth." He offered her a fraught smile. "I want you to know that I love Lindy with all my heart, and I'll do whatever I can to fix this. I want to marry her on Saturday."

Ruth stepped forward and hugged him tightly, saying on a sob, "We know that, Alex. We want that too."

Brady said, "Alex and Lindy need to sort this out between them. Tonight. Without any interference from anyone."

"I'm not sure Lindy . . . ," Ruth began.

"She doesn't have time to mess around. This has got to stop now." Brady had his ship captain's face and voice on again. "Come on, mate." He nodded toward the door to the house. Alex drew a deep breath and gripped the handle.

"Lindy's on the verandah," said Ruth.

Brady and Dave followed Alex inside.

"What about dinner?" cried Phil plaintively as Phoebe and Ruth followed the boys.

Kate and Sophie had disappeared. Angela sat on the couch, flipping through a magazine. Lindy was still alone, sitting like a statue on the verandah in the gathering dusk.

"Go," said Brady to Alex.

Angela made to stand up, but Dave gestured for her to stay and sat beside her. Alex closed the sliding door behind him. Brady pulled the vertical blinds.

"No one goes out there," he said. "And those two don't come in until they're happy again."

"Gosh." Phoebe exchanged glances with Ruth, who looked ready to force her way past Brady. He crinkled his forehead at her, and she changed her mind and went to the kitchen.

"We may as well eat," she said.

Phoebe stood uncertainly for a moment. Brady was completely serious. He wouldn't let Alex and Lindy back into the house until they behaved themselves. He wanted the marriage to go ahead as much as everyone else did. She moistened her lips, ready to start in on an apology.

"Is Alex back?" Kate's voice whipped through the silence. She and Sophie strode into the living area, ready to go to battle against men.

"He's talking to Lindy." Ruth frowned a warning at her daughter.

"Alone?" Sophie wasn't up for warnings.

"Yes."

"Trying to weasel his way out if it, no doubt," she said.

"Out of what?" asked Brady. His stern gray eyes clamped down on her.

"His lies."

Ruth's voice startled them all with its vehemence. "Don't you say things like that, Sophie. Alex is a good, decent man, and Lindy loves him. He loves her. What he's done in the past has no bearing on how he feels about Lindy and this wedding as far as Phil and I are concerned. We don't want you making things worse with remarks like that, thank you."

Sophie's cheeks turned a dull pink. Her aggressiveness deflated under a mother's wrath. "I'm sorry, Ruth."

Ruth's mouth twisted in a grim little smile. "We're all upset. Just remember, Alex is still the same man he was yesterday, even today, before any of this happened. You liked him then."

Brady said, "If I ever have a mother-in-law, Ruth, I hope she's like you." Phoebe blinked. *Mother-in-law? Brady?* He caught her astonished expression. "Theoretically speaking," he added, and turned away blank-faced to sit with Dave and Angela.

Of course. In theory. After this debacle, his warped opinion of weddings and marriage would be doubly reinforced.

About twenty minutes after Brad had given his ultimatum, Lindy and Alex, smiling and clutching hands, banged on the door and begged to be allowed to reenter the house. No one was keen to have a late night. The aftermath of the near calamity permeated the atmosphere like a damp fog. After dinner, Kate and Sophie piled into Dave and Angela's car, and Lindy and Alex went in Alex's, leaving Brady to Phoebe. The two troublemakers. *Outcasts.*

"Looks like I'm with you," he said. By his expression, she gathered he'd rather walk than ride with her.

"Fine." She didn't have much choice. Neither did he. They were both in trouble for the time being.

Two more days, that was all. He'd be out of the house by Sunday. She'd be back in her cottage with her new job to look forward to and the remains of the long weekend to enjoy. Saturday would be fully occupied with the wedding. Brady, the prickle in her sock, would be out of her life for good.

He got in and slammed the door. Fred's engine complained as she accelerated up the steep driveway, the car bouncing and leaping on loose stones to the access road. Brady gripped the handhold on the door but didn't comment on her driving.

She turned onto the smooth tarmac of Flying Fox Lane. "I'm sorry."

"For?" His voice was cool. An apology wouldn't mean much from her, probably, but it was one she needed to make, had been trying to make since he'd locked the traumatized couple out on the verandah.

"For saying you didn't want Lindy and Alex to get married. It was unfair and wrong. I'm sorry."

"Accepted." He said it so carelessly.

There was nothing more to say. She drove to the house in silence. When the Beetle was neatly parked next to Dave's sedan under an arching tree, Brady said, "Thanks for the ride."

"No problem."

She locked Fred and dropped her keys into her bag. Cool night air caressed her skin. Thousands of stars twinkled silvery light overhead. They were distant, untouchable, as remote from her as he was. She didn't want to go inside just yet. No one had really forgiven her for the ruckus. Lindy and Alex said they had, but there was a chill that hadn't been there before, the sense she'd interfered where she wasn't welcome, intruded into something private between them and exposed it for public display. Lindy might never forgive her for almost ruining her wedding day.

Brady didn't head straight for the house as she expected. He waited until she came around the car.

"I'm sorry too, Phoebe."

"Why?"

"It was my stupid remark that started the whole thing."

She sighed, couldn't think of anything to say here in the starlight with Brady standing so close. Moonlight and starlight had extraordinary effects, softening harsh edges, blunting hard words, smoothing angular contours. And enhancing memories—of kisses, embraces, soft words and firm arms, warm bodies.

How could he be so sensitive and tender and so insensitive at the same time?

"I should've known better than to make that type of joke with you," he said.

Joke? He still didn't get it.

"It's no joke," she snapped.

The pale oval of his face loomed over her. "If you'd taken it in the spirit it was intended, there wouldn't have been any problem at all."

"So it's my fault again now, is it?"

"We're both at fault." He sighed, but he didn't walk away. "It's over now. Can't we forget it?"

"I can."

"Good. Let's go in."

Phoebe hesitated. He paused, waiting.

"Come on. We'll face the music together."

So he felt the same chill she did. *Good.* She followed his dark bulk to the front door.

Everyone was drinking tea in the lounge area. Alex, sitting next to Lindy on the sofa, looked up. "Tea's just made. On the bench."

"Thanks." Phoebe poured two cups, handed one to Brady, and sat down next to him, her heart pounding. If there was going to be a showdown, it would be now. Lindy hadn't said a word to her privately; neither had Alex. No one had wanted to further upset Ruth and Phil during dinner, where the rather forced casual but relieved conversation had revolved around the imminent arrival of Lindy and Kate's grandparents.

Lindy didn't waste time.

"Why did you do it, Phoebe?"

Phoebe swallowed. She placed her teacup carefully on the coffee table. "When Brady told me, my immediate concern was ensuring Alex wasn't about to become a bigamist. It's my job," she said, forestalling Sophie, who'd opened her mouth to blurt something guaranteed to be unhelpful. "After that was resolved, my concern was you, Lindy." She moistened her lips. "I thought you should know."

"I thought if anyone should tell you, Alex should," interrupted Brady. "So I told Phoebe not to say anything. We agreed to talk to Alex about it first."

"It was a difficult situation." Angela spoke softly. "I don't know what I would have done."

"I don't think it's difficult at all," cried Kate. "Who cares if Alex did something crazy fifteen years ago? If he suddenly produced a wife and half a dozen kids, it'd be different." She snorted with laughter.

"We've resolved it now." Alex slipped his arm around Lindy's shoulders and drew her closer for a kiss. "I was wrong. I should have told her ages ago."

Phoebe blinked back a tear. "I'm so relieved."

"We all are. So how did you convince her to forgive you?" Kate grinned at Alex and her sister.

"I asked her if she'd ever done anything stupid and rash that she regretted."

"Alex!" Lindy gave him a little shove. "You promised not to tell."

"I won't." They clutched hands and smiled into each other's eyes.

"What? You've never done anything stupid and rash in your life!" Kate sat up straight, eyes bright, ready to pounce like a cat on a plaything.

Sophie stared. "Have you? I'm the rash, crazy one, not you."

To Phoebe's amazement, Lindy's face slowly took on the color of a stoplight.

"I have, but I'm not telling."

"And neither am I," said Alex.

"I've never told anyone else, and I never will, so you can forget about trying to make me." Lindy stood up. "I'm going to bed. Good night." She bent and kissed Alex.

"Me too." Angela rose as well.

"Not fair, Sis," wailed Kate as Lindy departed. She slumped back against the cushions. "What could she have done? And when? I wonder if Mum and Dad know."

"For heaven's sake, don't start something now. Wait till they're safely married," said Dave.

"You can come in now, Mr. Winters."

Brady dropped the *National Geographic* onto the magazine table. *At last!* He followed Graeme Tucker down the corridor and into the surgery, stomach tensed, legs stupidly weak. Dentists' offices all smelled the same. Why was that? And what was it? Fear mixed with mouthwash?

"Take a seat, please." Tucker indicated the reclining chair. "Phoebe tells me your tooth has been painful for several days and is getting worse. Is that correct?"

"Yes, almost a week now." Brady arranged himself awkwardly in the narrow seat, gripping the arms as he was tilted slowly backward. Classical music burbled softly from a player in the corner. A large round floodlight hovered above him, and beyond that, a mobile with little colored dragons revolved slowly, to take kids' minds off what was happening. He'd need more than a few papier-mâché dragons for that.

"I'm really grateful you could see me at short notice."

Thank heavens Phoebe wasn't there. The red-haired dental assistant clipped a paper bib around his neck. She smiled her professional, "relax the patient" smile. Phoebe would be good at that bit. She had a lovely smile. It was the first thing he'd noticed about her. What was she doing, anyway? She'd gone off with the girls after lunch. Alex had dropped him for his appointment.

"We had a cancellation. You were lucky. Now, which tooth are we looking at?"

"Upper right rear."

The light clicked on, and the dentist's masked face appeared in his field of vision.

"Open, please."

Brady obeyed. The door opened and closed. Female voices

murmured. He couldn't move to see what was happening behind him; the dentist had him pinned with some probe thing in his mouth, scraping and poking happily.

"Mmm. I see quite a buildup of plaque, Mr. Winters." There was more scraping, then a blinding jab of pain.

"Aaaoooowwwhhhh." Perspiration beaded Brady's brow. His breath came in rapid, shallow gasps.

"Sorry. I think I found the culprit." The dentist gave a dry little chuckle. He continued his exploration, humming along to the music, then removed the probe. "We'll do an X-ray of that sucker."

He retreated from view. Brady stared at the dragons in an attempt to blot out the throbbing pain. His fingertips had gone numb, and he eased his clawed hands off the armrests. If Brady wasn't such a gentleman, Tucker would be flat on his back with his own dental problems—missing teeth.

"Put these on, please." It was a gentle, very familiar voice.

Phoebe! *Here? Why didn't she say?* There she was, smiling in her dental uniform and holding out a pair of yellow-rimmed dark glasses. He groaned and jammed the specs on. Why not complete the hideous experience by having Phoebe witness his humiliation and pain? She'd love it. And so would the other girls when she related her tale.

Tucker hove into view again. "I think we'll do a full X-ray of your mouth. I'm assuming you haven't had one done recently?"

"No."

"Just as well to check everything while we have you here in captivity, as it were. On dry land." He gave another little laugh, accompanied by a familiar giggle from Brady's left. No wonder Tucker liked Phoebe: she laughed at his rotten jokes. "We'd feel pretty silly if we developed an abscess in a different tooth six months down the track, wouldn't we?"

Brady grunted. *We certainly couldn't feel any sillier than we do right now.*

"Open, please." Something hard and angular was inserted into his right cheek. A machine took aim at his jaw. "Bite down carefully. Hold." Buzzzzzz. The process was repeated on the left side.

"This is an interesting case, Phoebe," said Tucker. "We're lucky to have one during your training. Look at this."

There was muttering from behind; then Tucker loomed over him again. "Well, Mr. Winters, I'll begin treatment on that tooth today. I need to clean out the decay before an abscess can develop. I can do some of the work now, but you'll need to return in a week's time to complete the treatment."

"A week?" His scrambled brain vaguely remembered Phoebe mentioning something about having to stay on.

"I'm afraid so. There's other work to be done as well. I can see three more teeth heading for trouble if we don't do fillings, and you need a scale and clean, but you won't want everything done at once, and I doubt I can fit you into my schedule immediately, anyway. You'll need to talk to Felicity to arrange those appointments over the next few weeks. How does that sound?"

Horrible! Torture! "Inevitable, I suppose." Brady moistened his dry lips. "Can you relieve the pain?" Did he sound as feeble and weakly pleading as he felt?

"For the most part, yes."

A soft, warm hand closed over his left, squeezed briefly, and let go. *Sweet girl.*

An hour later Phoebe led a stunned and numb Brady to the Beetle. What a horrendous procedure. He'd never had his mouth open for so long. His jaw was aching from the strain. Good thing Tucker didn't hold a grudge. Biting his finger had been a complete accident and purely because Brady couldn't prevent any longer his jaw from snapping closed.

"I had no idea what a root canal was. It sounded bad enough, and it looked even worse. I don't know how you stood that," she said.

"Neither do I."

"Does it hurt?"

"It's still numb from the anesthetic. My whole jaw feels like dead rubber." He poked at it with one finger.

"Graeme's great, isn't he?" she asked brightly. "It was nice of him to let me go early to take you home." She flung her car door open and leaned across to open his side.

"Yes. A real charmer."

"Funny the way he hums while he works."

"Hilarious."

He lowered himself into the passenger seat with a sigh of relief. He felt no pain for the first time in a week. That was a blessing. He wasn't allowed to eat for a few hours, but he'd never felt less like eating in his life. Tucker said to take analgesics when the anesthetic wore off because Brady "could be in some discomfort." Discomfort he could take—anything but that excruciating pain.

"You'll be able to enjoy the wedding now."

He turned a jaundiced eye her way and met that lovely beaming smile she'd worn on the first day—the one he'd destroyed within hours of their meeting and seen briefly once since.

He managed a feeble half-numb but heartfelt grin. He probably looked like a stroke victim, all lopsided and slack on one side. Was he dribbling? He wiped his numb mouth just in case. "Yes. We both will."

A few minutes later she said, "You'll have to find somewhere to stay."

"I'll book into a motel."

"Mmm. Might be difficult this time of year."

A little worm of alarm crept through the fog in his battered mind. "Surely there'll be somewhere?"

"Maybe. You'll probably find a room for a few days here and there. You might have to keep moving, that's all. Hard to find somewhere for a couple of weeks straight. And remember this is the Australia Day long weekend."

"Is it?" Australia Day, January 26, hadn't entered his head for years. The wedding was January 24. It still hadn't clicked, even when he was making flight bookings.

"Yes. All the guests were told to book their accommodations well in advance, and they're only staying one or two nights."

"I wasn't told to do that."

"You didn't need to, because Lindy had the house lined up."

"And I was supposed to leave on Sunday," he finished mournfully. "I suppose I really *do* have to stay?" Maybe Tucker was being extra careful. Maybe that other work wasn't really necessary.

Phoebe stamped on those vain hopes. "Yes, unless you've got a dentist who will take you on and finish the treatment, which you said you don't. You'd have to stay in one place over there, anyway, until it was completed."

"I don't suppose Ruth and Phil can fit me in with all the relatives staying there."

Phoebe couldn't believe what she was hearing. She thought she'd be free of him in just a few days. "I don't know. See how you go with motels first." Should she offer her spare room? *No.* Too small. Too jammed full of stuff. Too intimate. She'd planned her resistance to him only until Sunday. Longer exposure than that would be . . . trouble. Even though he was in pain and needy. Especially because he was in pain and needy. *No, definitely not!*

Phoebe swung into the driveway, stopped in her usual spot under the tree, and pulled on the hand brake. Poor Brady. He really was a miserable specimen at the moment. She opened the car door. The enticing aroma of barbecuing fish permeated the air around the house. Someone was already cooking dinner.

"Mmm. Smells good," she said.

"I'm not allowed to eat."

"Oh dear. Poor you."

She led the walking wounded through to the verandah, where everyone was relaxing, watching Dave control the monster barbecue down on the paved area.

"How's the tooth, mate?" Dave asked.

"Numb." Brady sagged onto a recliner and lay back with his eyes closed. Graeme had said he'd need care and rest after the procedure, because the anesthetic was strong and made people woozy. When it started to wear off, he'd need painkillers. "Lucky you've got Phoebe to look after you," he'd said to Brady, who hadn't looked particularly pleased by that stroke of luck. He wouldn't want to stay at her house either. No need to feel guilty about not offering.

She said, "He had an emergency root canal, and he needs to go back next week to have the work finished properly. After that, he has an appointment two weeks later."

"So you have to stay three more weeks?" Lindy's expression was all sympathy. "Can you do that? What about your boat?"

"Where will you stay?" chimed in Kate. "You can't use this place, because the owners are due home on Sunday night. We have to have a big cleanup on Sunday morning."

"And Mum and Dad have all the grandees staying."

"It's all right. I'll find a motel."

"You'll be lucky." Kate pulled a face.

"There's sure to be something for a night or two." He turned an anguished face to Phoebe for reassurance. "Won't there?" He couldn't drive, operate heavy machinery, make important decisions, drink alcohol or hot drinks, eat, or do a few other things she'd forgotten.

"After the holidays are over, in February, you'll be fine," she said. "Narooma empties out then."

"I'll start phoning right now." Lindy jumped up and strode into the house.

"What's she doing?" Now he was totally bewildered, poor boy. He wasn't used to having decisions made for him; he was more used to giving the orders.

"She's looking for a place for you to stay," said Alex. "Lindy's a terrific organizer. She'll manage something."

"Oh, she didn't need to . . . doesn't have to . . ." His eyes closed, and he winced.

"Don't worry, mate. You're our best man. She'll take care of it."

But fifteen minutes later, she came back with a worried face to sit with everyone at the outdoor table, where Dave's cooked fish was steaming gently in its foil wrapping, ready for eating.

"I got you into the Ocean View next Wednesday for a week. It's upmarket, but all the cheaper places are gone. After that, you can either move or stay on. There are more options then, and you can choose."

"What about from Sunday to Tuesday?"

"Absolutely nothing Sunday and Monday. I'm sorry. There's some sort of car enthusiasts rally thing here over the weekend on top of the normal holidays, and it's the last long weekend in summer. Tuesday you can have a room at the Crest. I booked that."

"Thanks, Lindy. You're fantastic." He offered a weak smile.

"Not really. It was only a matter of phoning around." Her brain was still working on the problem. Phoebe knew the signs. Lindy wasn't going to give up until Brady had a bed. "All I can think of for the missing nights is Phoebe's place. Phoebe? You have a spare room, don't you?" All eyes swung to her.

"Umm. Not really—well, yes, sort of . . ." Crunch time. Did she want Brady in her house? No. Not at all. He was too big and overwhelming. Her house was small. Her spare room was stuffed full of books and a desk and . . . things.

"It's an emergency," said Alex.

"It's only a couple of nights." *Very helpful, Kate.*

"I suppose . . ."

"I'd be eternally grateful, Phoebe," Brady said. And she might be eternally sorry. But it would be churlish to refuse. Where else could he go?

"All right." Was it? "But it's not very big. In fact, it's a tiny room, and there's a heap of stuff in it, because I packed things away while the renters are in."

He reached out a hand and squeezed hers, stopping the flow of words and her brain with a gentle, warm "Thank you."

"Perfect!" Lindy clapped her hands.

"When are you three going to Phil and Ruth's?" asked Alex.

"After dinner, nine-ish, I told them."

"Does it really take all day to get three women ready for a wedding?" Dave stacked his plate with potato salad. "Plus a sleepover the night before?"

"No seeing the bride on the wedding day until the wedding. You know that," said Angela. "It's so exciting."

"We need an early start," said Sophie. "The hairdresser is coming at eight."

"But the wedding's not till four!"

"Stop stirring, Dave." Angela poked him.

"At least if you're already on the premises, you won't be late," said Alex.

Lindy kissed his cheek. "I won't be late, don't you worry, after all the effort it's taken to get us this far."

Chapter Eight

How are you feeling, mate?"

Brady cocked an eye at Alex, who was sitting beside him in the backseat of Dave's car, looking uncomfortably swish in his suit.

"Still time to back out and do a runner," called Dave from the driver's seat.

"He doesn't want to do a runner, do you, Alex?" Angela smiled over her shoulder at him.

"I'm fine." Alex certainly looked happy.

"I'm the last free man standing," said Brady.

"Don't you want to settle down?" Angela asked.

"I'm having too good a time to be stuck in one place."

"Lucky sod."

"You made your choice, Dave, too late now," Angela said. "How's your tooth, Brady?"

"It's sore from that operation and my whole jaw aches. Different pain but still bad."

"Phoebe says that dentist is very good."

"He was all right, but I bit his finger. He was a bit frosty after that."

"Mate, I wouldn't be game to go back," cried Alex as, predictably enough, they all erupted into fits of laughter. "He'll have spent the week coming up with something really nasty."

Why did they all think it was so funny? Phoebe didn't. Neither did Tucker. "I didn't mean to. I just couldn't keep my mouth open any longer. He might be used to it."

"Glad he doesn't hold a grudge, that's all I can say."

Phil and Ruth's house had been transformed since their last visit.

A marquee sheltered the back patio area, decorated with tubs and baskets of flowers. Catering staff moved around inside, setting tables. Several small children ran about the garden under the eye of a gray-haired woman in purple, ensuring they didn't drown in the lake. She turned and waved when she saw them unloading from the car.

"Aunt Sarah," said Alex.

Phoebe's Beetle rolled in next to Dave's car, nose to the fence. Several cars with interstate plates were lined up already. Brady waited for her while Angela, Alex, and Dave headed for the house and the enthusiastic welcome from Aunt Sarah and assorted leaping children.

"Pink suits you," he said as Phoebe joined him. Her celebrant's dress was demure but elegant in a soft pastel shade that highlighted her skin and hair color. Like strawberry cream. Good enough to eat.

"Thank you. A suit suits you."

"I don't wear one often. Not with a tailcoat, like this."

"You all *look* very refined." The teasing emphasis implied that the refinement was superficial.

"We do scrub up pretty well." He laughed. "But don't expect any other changes."

The others disappeared into the house.

"The marquee looks great. Are you nervous about your best man speech?"

"Yes, it does look good, and no, I'm not nervous. Dave and I are doing a double act." Brady stopped. He held her gently by the elbow. "Phoebe? Are you really all right with my staying at your house? You kind of got pushed into it. . . . Lindy is very persuasive."

She smiled. "I know."

"I can sleep on the floor here if you'd rather. I don't mind, and I'm sure Phil and Ruth won't."

"It's fine. It's only two nights." She slipped her arm from his grasp and opened the door onto a room packed with well-dressed chattering people. It wasn't a very convincing response. Brady sucked in a deep breath, stretched his mouth into a smile, and followed her.

* * *

"So here I am, the last single member of the Brotherhood." His arm around Dave's shoulders, Brady gazed at the assembled guests as he wound up their speech. "We three vowed we'd stick together through thick and thin, and we have. Now they're entering a new phase of their lives, but we'll always be best mates."

"Hear! Hear!" cried Dave. "Nothing comes in the way of our friendship. I know Lindy was a little . . . shall we say . . . disturbed by the prospect of the Brotherhood reunited." He waited while the laughter and rude interjections, not least from Alex, died down. "But she needn't be. She's part of the team now, like Ange is and like Brady's future wife will be, whoever she may be."

"No, no, mate," interrupted Brady. "Beautiful as Lindy and Angela are, as terrific as they are, marriage is not for me. I couldn't be happier for my two best mates, and I know they couldn't be happier with their chosen wives." He paused, glanced around the crowded marquee, caught Phoebe's eye, looked away quickly. "If I ever find a girl like either of those two women, I might have to rethink."

There were cheers and applause. Dave slapped him on the back.

"We're supposed to be toasting two other lovely women, Brady. Kate and Sophie, Lindy's bridesmaids. Kate, by all accounts the pesky little sister who has grown up into a beautiful young woman, and Sophie, Lindy's best friend, who may have been a pesky little sister to someone once, but is a beautiful young woman too."

Brady raised his glass. In it was sparkling mineral water. He'd never toasted anyone with water before. "To the bridesmaids," he said in unison with Dave.

"To the bridesmaids," roared the crowd. Brady and Dave clinked glasses, then sat down. People began moving about between tables, talking and laughing. Alex's uncle, on Phoebe's left, excused himself and went off to talk to the newlyweds.

"Excuse me, dear. I'm Lindy's great-aunt. It was a beautiful service."

Phoebe turned. The elderly relative hovered at her side, smiling.

"Thank you. I love celebrating weddings, and it's even more special when my friends are involved."

"What a wonderful job you have. Thank you." The lady moved on.

It had gone well. All her research had paid off; all the little secrets she'd winkled out of the boys and Kate and Sophie about the happy couple had raised plenty of laughter and good cheer. The innocent secrets. Not the big ones, such as how close this had come to being a disaster. She closed her eyes in a silent thank-you to whichever god had intervened.

"Hey, smile! They're safely hitched, and you did a great job." Brady slid into the empty chair next to her.

"Thanks. It's such a relief." She blew air out in a whoosh and shook her head. He really did look extremely handsome in a suit. Broad shoulders, straight back, and lean athletic body showed off the tailoring to perfection. Of the three, he was by far the best-looking. Her eyes had kept straying his way during the service. Shameful when the celebrant couldn't keep her eyes off the best man. No one had noticed as far as she knew.

"Tell me about it." He hitched the chair legs away from an uneven piece of ground, closer to her.

Now he was acting as if they'd been side by side in the trenches when in reality he'd been more furious with her than Alex and Lindy had. But Brady when he was being nice was dangerous. She mustn't stare. She'd made a terrible mistake allowing him to stay. Two days. How would she stand it?

"How's the pain?"

"Increasing. I'll need another pill soon. At least I was able to eat."

"You and Dave were great with your double act. You speak well in public."

"Thanks."

"I read once that most people would rather jump out of a plane than talk to a crowd like this."

"I wouldn't."

"Me neither."

"I'd rather speak in public than go to the dentist."

Phoebe laughed. "And you have two more visits."

He groaned theatrically. "At least the pain will be gone. That was unbearable. Like a spike through the head."

"What will you do in your time here?"

"Heaven only knows. I'm not used to doing nothing."

"Look on it as a holiday. Narooma is a very popular spot."

"I don't take holidays."

"Never?"

"Not usually. My whole life is like a holiday."

"Lucky you." Carefree and irresponsible. Except he was the captain of a ship, so someone must think he was responsible—the owners. The boat must be worth millions.

"But that's what I meant, Phoebe, when I asked you what you really wanted to do with your life. You should do something you love."

"Well, I don't have that luxury. Except doing these . . ." She waved her arm around, indicating the wedding celebrations. "But I don't earn enough to live off it, and I'm not usually a guest. Next Saturday I have three in a row. Two here and one in Central Tilba in the morning. "

"Can I come?"

Her gaze whipped to his face with a snort of astonished laughter. "To the weddings? Why? You hate weddings."

"Not to the weddings—to Central Tilba. I'll need to get out of town by then. I'll be stir-crazy."

She shrugged. "If you like. It's a nice little place. Full of arty-crafty shops and ones selling cheese and honey."

"Good. Do you own your house?"

That was a quick change of tack. Or was he still on the "doing something you love" topic? Was it his business? And why did he want to know? Still . . . it was no secret.

"Yes. I inherited it from Gran."

"That's a big plus."

"I know, but it doesn't mean I don't need a job. Owning a house is very expensive. Taxes and all that. And it needs a lot of repairs."

"Maybe I can help you with those while I'm here." His expression brightened.

"Oh no, you don't need to . . ."

"I won't have anything to do, and I get bored very easily." Now he was sitting up straight, eager and ready to grab a hammer and start fixing things.

"Umm."

"I'm very handy." He was almost pleading. "I can carpenter, do plumbing, paint . . . pretty much anything."

"I'm sure you can. It's not that."

"What, then?"

What indeed? Brady's making himself at home in her house, making himself indispensable, a fixture, something she could get used to. A man around the place. A handsome man. *That* man. "I . . . nothing. I'll think about it. Thank you." It was only two days and a trip to Central Tilba and back. She'd survive.

Phoebe stuck the key in the lock and pushed the front door open. Her tenants had left a few hours earlier and should have cleaned as thoroughly as the wedding party had done all morning in the other house. It looked okay superficially. An odd smell hung in the air. Brady stepped in behind her, lugging his duffel and a carry bag of leftover food from the group house.

"Nice," he said. "Cozy. I like the front verandah."

"You mean small." She left her bag on the floor and opened the windows.

"No, I don't. I mean nice and cozy." He dumped his bag on a chair. "I live on a boat, remember."

"Your room is along there. I'll have to clear stuff out first." She pointed down the corridor to the spare room. "The bathroom is here, kitchen through there. Make yourself at home."

"Funny smell," he said. "Is that normal?"

"No."

She took her own bag into her bedroom. The people had stripped the bed and presumably put the used linen in the laundry. Glancing into the bathroom on the way to the spare room, she found everything clean and sparkling.

Brady was in the kitchen, filling the electric kettle. "Tea?"

"Yes, please."

"I think they cooked smelly food. It's stronger in here, but the garbage is empty. Probably just needs airing."

She unlocked the spare room.

Brady hovered behind her. "Are you planning to lock me in?"

"I had a lock put on specially for the rental. I locked away my CDs and personal stuff. I use this as an office."

"And storeroom. There's a bed under there somewhere, I suppose." He crowded past her to the bed laden with teetering piles of stuff. A piece of silver tinsel dangled from a green plastic bin-liner bag. "Christmas decorations."

"I warned you."

"No problem. What's in here?" He peered into a cardboard box. "Your spare dinner service?"

"It was Gran's china. I don't have room for it anywhere else."

"You like jigsaws, I see. I may have to borrow a couple." He lifted the first boxes off a stack of a dozen and looked at the pictures. "Montmartre. The Taj Mahal. That looks hard. All that blue sky."

"Gran loved doing them. I still have a lot of her things."

He grabbed a cardboard box full of books and looked about for a spot to put it. There wasn't space on the floor, not where he wouldn't trip over it constantly. She'd moved the vacuum cleaner into the laundry. Under the bed was full too. He wouldn't need drawer or wardrobe space for a two-night stay luckily.

"I was going to take those to the bookshop. Put them on the deck out the back."

"Right." He disappeared.

Phoebe picked up a pile of sweaters and a coat she'd dumped on the bed for want of a better place and took them to her bedroom. Brady came back. "I like the deck too. Great view."

"Yes."

"This place has a lot of potential." He moved a suitcase full of Gran's linen from the end of the bed. "Deck?"

"Yes. And this." She handed him a big stuffed-full red-and-blue-striped blanket bag.

"I can see the bed now." He went out whistling.

She cleared the top of her desk and the dressing table, ramming all the bits and pieces into already full drawers. She'd have to trust Brady not to poke into her private affairs, the papers in her desk, the photographs and letters. He wouldn't. She did trust him in that way, she realized.

The teakettle shrieked in the kitchen. His footsteps echoed in the corridor, and the sound subsided. Phoebe found a duster and wiped down the exposed surfaces. She took the quilt off the bed and hung it over the railing on the deck to air. He could make his own bed. She collected a towel and sheets for both their beds.

"Tea's up," he called. "Out on the deck."

He'd found mugs and biscuits and set them on the rickety old cane table.

"I put those veggies and things away. We'll have to go to the shops. This is the last of the milk we brought home, and we need bread," he said.

"There's a corner store a couple of blocks along. Round the corner, down the hill, and then to the left."

"I'll go after tea. Give you some space to settle in."

"Thanks."

"You really have a great spot here." He sipped his tea and gazed out at the view of the hinterland. A group of green-and-red parrots hopped about in the tree hanging over the back fence. "Good being up on the rise so you get the sea view from the front and the hills from the back. How old's the house?"

"Built in the forties, I think. Gran fixed up the kitchen and bathroom a bit but, as you can see, not much else." He'd have to be blind to miss the peeling paint around the window frames and the worn boards and wobbly railing on the front steps, and out here, the deck needed restaining. Plus there were water stains on the kitchen walls and ceiling where the roof had leaked in that freak storm the previous year. John from next door said the guttering needed replacing.

"The land would be worth a fair bit."

"Probably. But I'm not thinking of selling." What was he saying but not saying?

"I'm not suggesting you do."

She put her mug of tea down carefully on the table. "Brady, I'm happy here. I like my life, and I like my house. Whether you think I'm wasting my life, compromising, or however you put it, whether I should move away, or sell because my house is on a good piece of land—all of that—what you think—is completely irrelevant to me."

"You're not protesting too much, are you?"

"What?" A couple of parrots flew up in alarm at her screech. "You're impossible." She folded her arms tightly across her chest. He laughed, and she turned to glare at him, furious at his nonchalance and the way he managed to imply she was an overreacting, under-achieving fool of a woman. "You come swanning into my life, lose me my job, upset my best friend and nearly break up her wedding . . ."

"You did that," he interjected. He was still laughing at her, she could tell, even though he wasn't actually smiling. His mouth had a suspicious twitch to it.

"No, *you* did! If you hadn't been here, none of it would have happened."

"And your life would have continued on, dull as ever, until you died of old age or boredom, whichever came first."

"Why does life have to be constantly exciting? Some of us like peace and quiet and stability."

"There'll be plenty of time for that when you're dead." He stood up and collected the tea things. "I'll go to the shop now in case my death is more imminent than I think." With a chortle of laughter, he went into the house.

He had that right! Phoebe's fingers itched to get around his throat. He was so big and complacent and sure of himself. Growling, she sprang off her chair and went to unpack. If he kept that act up, she'd have no trouble resisting him till Tuesday.

Brady sauntered down the sloping street to the corner store. He shouldn't tease Phoebe, but she was wasting herself. Not that Narooma was an inherently bad place to live—quite the contrary. It was a beautiful spot, especially if you were involved with boats and the sea.

He'd wander along to the little harbor and see what was what in the next few days, maybe take a tour out to Montague Island. Phil said there was a charter company operating here that ran day trips, fishing charters, and whale-watching excursions. It wouldn't be anything like his own company. This mob would cater to a whole different crowd. It would be satisfying nonetheless. It was the ocean life that interested him, not the money, and certainly not the social-class angle. Many of the clients who could afford to charter *Lady Lydia* were unbelievable pains in the bum, and quite a few didn't know how close they'd come to being tossed overboard after some rude and exotic display of arrogance towards him or his crew.

The lady behind the counter rang up his purchases with a cheery smile. A streak of purple brightened her steely gray hair. "Enjoying your stay?"

"Yes, thanks."

"Are you at the Ocean View?" That was the holiday apartment block just over the crest of the hill. She probably did quite well from them. The name sounded familiar. Was that where Lindy had booked the week? He'd walk along and check.

"No, with a friend."

"A local?"

"Yes." Would she go so far as to ask who? He waited while she packed his bread and milk into a bag, taking great care over the precise placement of each item. She was obviously busting to know who he was visiting.

"Who would that be?" And had no qualms about asking.

"Phoebe Curtis."

"Oh, lovely." Was Phoebe lovely or was the fact that he was staying there? Whatever her meaning, her interest level had skyrocketed.

"Yes." That covered both. And Phoebe *was* lovely.

"Staying long?" She handed him the bag and leaned her hip comfortably against the counter, arms folded. The fingers of both hands sported chunky silver rings with massive assorted gemstones.

"Only till Tuesday with Phoebe. Then I'm moving to a motel for a few weeks."

"That's a shame."

"Is it?" He studied her with a serious expression but allowed a tiny smile to lurk, instead of laughing aloud, which he really wanted to do.

"Oh . . . no. I mean . . ."

Two new customers entered the shop and headed for the frozen food.

She leaned over the counter with a conspiratorial frown and a lowered voice. "I think Phoebe gets lonely there all by herself. I knew her gran. Edna was a crabby old thing. . . ." The purple flash in her hair shook with the memory. "She grumbled about any little thing she could think of. Poor Phoebe couldn't put a foot right. Poor girl. And she's so sweet. Looked after the old woman right till the end, and never a complaining word out of her. She has no one, you know."

The accusing look she gave him sent an unaccustomed pang of remorse for his teasing shooting to his core.

"Yes. I wonder . . ." He gazed around the crowded shelves of the little shop. "Do you have some nice chocolates?"

"Nothing really special, I'm afraid. Just these." She indicated a shelf with several colored boxes. "But Phoebe will enjoy anything. She's partial to chocolate. And every girl loves being given a treat from a handsome man." She sniggered.

Brady grinned and winked. "I'd better get something for dinner while I'm here." He selected the most expensive chocolates, imported from Belgium, and grabbed a bottle of ready-made pasta sauce and a packet of spaghetti. They'd brought enough salad stuff home from the other house.

He waited while she served the other customers, then placed his new items on the counter.

She smirked. "Do you cook too? You're quite a catch."

"No one's caught me yet."

"Yet." She chuckled again. "Give her time."

"Who?"

"Phoebe, of course."

"Phoebe doesn't want to catch me, that's for sure. I've done nothing but upset her since I arrived."

"Oh well. You'd better start making up for it, then, hadn't you? Phoebe's a special girl. You'd be mad to let her get away."

"Thanks. I'll keep it in mind. Good-bye." Brady grabbed up his carry bag and made a dash for the safety of the street. Was that normal? Would everyone he met be on intimate terms with Phoebe's personal life? Maybe not. That lady had probably seen her almost every day for years, and having known the grandmother would give her even more inside knowledge. *Cripes.*

She'd winkled information out of him as easily as could be and was very free with her own. For all she knew, his and Phoebe's friendship was very slight and distant. Better move out on Tuesday or she'd have them married in no time. He'd forgotten how gossip worked in small country towns. Phoebe and her new friend would be the hot topic in the corner store for weeks after he left.

He wandered back up the hill. Opposite lay part of the golf

course. A few late stragglers lugged their buggies along. He'd get in a few rounds while he was here. The Narooma course had the best view in the world, running along the cliff tops, with the Pacific Ocean crashing and curling ceaselessly below. He paused to stare at the horizon, misty and indistinct now as the sun sank beneath the hills behind him. There'd be some glorious sunsets. Already a gold-and-reddish purple glow was enveloping everything. And the air was so fresh and clear. It was quiet, too, peaceful despite the busyness of the long weekend.

He'd better check his booking at that Ocean View place.

Phoebe heaved a sigh of relief when Brady left the house. She stowed away her clothes and sorted out things for washing the next day. He was such a pain, like having a prickle or an itch that constantly annoyed and wouldn't go away. Did he realize that? For sure he did. Telling her she'd have died of boredom if he hadn't come along! Too bad if he died of boredom during his stay in Narooma. It'd serve him right, the smug know-it-all. He'd have to slow down his jet-setting millionaire lifestyle and adjust to how normal people lived—peacefully and uneventfully, just the way she liked it.

She bundled up her dirty clothes and charged into the laundry. The washer was full of sheets and towels. *Right.* She dumped her load on the floor and started the machine. He could do his own washing.

What on earth could she offer him for dinner? If she'd been there by herself, she'd have had a sandwich or a boiled egg. Except there weren't any eggs. But anything would do for her, or she could nip down to Robyn's shop and get something. She should have thought to mention it when he went off for the milk. He'd just have to go back.

Would he settle for takeout pizza? He might have to.

He caused nothing but problems.

When the front door opened, Phoebe was in the kitchen, putting together a salad from the leftover food they'd brought home with them. Whatever they decided to eat, this was a start. A track from her *Chill-Out Sessions* CD wafted from the stereo. It was very soothing. She'd missed her own music the past week. She'd missed her little house. It was good to be home.

"Hi," he called. "It's me."

"In the kitchen."

Brady hoisted a plastic carry bag onto the bench. He pulled out milk and bread and put them away. She continued with her preparations, back turned.

"I got you this," he said. "To say sorry for teasing you and thank you for letting me stay."

He stood beside her, forcing her to look at his outstretched hand. Belgian chocolates. A big box.

"Oh! Thank you. I love those." She glanced at his face. Was that a hint of worry? Concern she might not like his gift?

"That's what the lady in the shop said." It was definitely a relieved smile he wore.

"Robyn."

"Purple streak?"

She nodded, unable to reply, too overcome with astonishment and remorse for her unkind, murderous thoughts.

"I mean it, Phoebe. I'm sorry for saying those things about your life here." He wanted a response, wanted reassurance from her. It was a bit late for that. Why didn't he simply stop making that type of remark? Then they'd both be happy.

And he could stop being so attractive while he was at it.

She nodded again. "Thanks," she managed to murmur. He was doing it again: overwhelming her with his presence, surprising her, knocking her sideways, throwing her off center, bowling her over, confusing her when she'd thought she'd sorted him out in her head. Making himself irresistible.

"I got this for our dinner," he said next. "You must have read my mind. That salad will be perfect with it. What a good team we are."

With a beaming smile, he plonked a packet of spaghetti and a bottle of ready-made Mediterranean sauce on the bench.

Chapter Nine

Phoebe laughed. "I was thinking takeaway pizza."

The smile disappeared in a flash. "Oh. Well—that's all right. This will keep."

"No, don't be stupid. I much prefer spaghetti. Pizza was a last resort."

The smile reappeared. "Easier on my tooth too."

Phoebe finished the salad and took out two saucepans. Brady picked a piece of lettuce from the salad bowl and leaned against the doorframe, chewing.

"What happened there?"

She followed his gaze to the water-stained ceiling and wall. "We had an almighty storm last year and the roof leaked. My neighbor says the gutters need replacing." She pulled a resigned face. No way would that be happening anytime soon.

"I can do that."

"Replace all the guttering?"

"Yes, why not?"

"Basically because I can't afford it."

"I'll do it for free."

"I can't afford any of it. Work or new gutters. And apparently the eaves are rotten in some places."

"I'll check it out tomorrow." He took more lettuce with a satisfied smile and resumed lounging.

"Thanks, but I really can't afford to replace anything at the moment. When I start getting paid from the new job, it'll be different, but it'll take months for me to get ahead and save enough."

"Don't worry about it. Let me pay for it."

"No!" Her whole body jerked in astonishment, and the saucepans clattered onto the stove top.

"As a loan if you like."

"No, no, no." A desperate lunge saved the larger pan from crashing to the floor.

"Why not?"

"Because . . ." She cast about desperately for the first and best reason, but there were so many objections she couldn't choose where to start.

"Because?" he prompted. "Because you don't have any good reasons."

"I have so many I can't choose."

"For instance?"

"I hardly know you."

"Rubbish. You know me better than any tradesman you'd pay to do it. And that's completely irrelevant, anyway."

"But you're not a tradesman and you're saying you'll do it for nothing. I can't take money from you."

"Okay. Lend me the Beetle while I'm here. I'll need a car. I was thinking of hiring one, but this will work well. You'll be at the dentist's all day. You won't need to drive. Payment in kind, it's called. Sounds like a good deal to me."

There was that confident expression again. All sorted, every angle covered to his satisfaction. What was wrong with this picture? Her mouth opened and closed as objections crowded into her head. Where to start?

"Unless you think I can't do the job properly."

"Can you?" Good point. And did he have a driver's license? He lived on a boat. How long had it been since he'd driven a car?

"Yes, or I wouldn't offer." That was most likely true. Brady wasn't a man who enjoyed failing and wouldn't place himself in that situation. "So can I?"

"No. I don't want you to. It's too much." She shook her head, frowning.

"All right. New gutters are out. What about paint? Can you afford a few tins of paint?"

"I think so."

"I'll do the window frames. They need sanding right back and starting again."

"Fine. If you'd like to do that. Thank you."

"Deal. I won't be able to get started until Tuesday unless you've got sandpaper. Have you got a ladder?"

"A stepladder. There might be sandpaper in the shed." Her brain was still grappling with the issue of letting him drive Fred; his brain was already computing the necessities of a painting binge.

"I'll check it out in the morning. And can I borrow the Beetle to transport the paint, please?"

"Can you drive?"

"Of course I can drive. I have an international license. It's easiest, because we visit so many countries."

He took her resigned sigh as the agreement it was and went off with a jaunty stride to the living room. Moments later the TV newsreader started telling them about a shark attack at the Gold Coast.

It was amazing how the prospect of a day's work brightened him. How much paint would he need to buy? How much did paint cost? And what about brushes? What color should she choose? They'd have to go together. But when? Lunchtime? He could at least bring back sample paint charts. No way was he picking colors for her house.

She filled the largest pan with water. Should she stay with the sky blue that hadn't been changed in thirty years? Cream walls and forest-green trim had always appealed. That would mean painting the whole house, or she'd have pale blue walls and dark green frames. Hideous.

And if she had the whole outside painted, what was the use without repairing the guttering first? At the first thunderstorm the walls would be stained again, and it rained a lot here. It was a catch-22. He couldn't possibly do all that work by himself in the few weeks he'd be there. How disappointing! Just when she'd started to warm to the idea of repainted frames . . .

She left the water to boil. He was in her favorite chair, watching the weather report on TV, and glanced up as she joined him.

"Hot again tomorrow."

"Yes, I could have told you that. Listen, Brady." She sucked in air. He'd be disappointed too, more so than she. He'd looked so cheerful, and now she was about to spoil his fun. "There's no point painting anything because if you go to that trouble I'd like a different color from blue but you'd have to paint the whole house or I'd end up with green frames and blue walls and that would be horrible but you won't have time to do it all and there's no point painting anything unless the gutters and eaves are fixed and I can't afford that so you can't paint anything."

He stared at her, blank-faced under the barrage of words. "Finished?"

She nodded, breathless.

"Are you saying you want to change the color scheme?"

"Yes, but you can't—"

He held up his hand. "Don't start that again."

"Well . . . don't you agree?" Her fingers had begun twisting themselves around each other. She pulled them apart and wiped her palms on her shorts.

He sat up straight and leaned forward, giving her all his attention. "I assume we're talking about the outside? What color do you want?"

"I've always thought creamy white walls and green trim would be nice."

"It would be, but what about a darker blue or even a greeny blue instead of green? That would work with both color schemes."

Dark blue? Off-white and blue? Very fresh and cheery. And if they chose the right blue, it would work with the current pale blue walls quite well. A smile crept across her face as she imagined the effect. Definitely better than the peeling flakes and bare timber she had now.

"Happy? Now go away and cook, or sit down and watch this next program. It's about Cuba. You said you like Cuba."

She shook her head. "I'd better check that the spaghetti water's not boiling dry."

The smile he gave her before she retreated to the kitchen sent a warm, tingling glow straight to her heart.

Brady enjoyed himself immensely on Tuesday. First thing he drove Phoebe to work at the dentist's under her eagle-eyed supervision.

"You don't think I can handle this car, do you?" he asked when she told him for the third time how sensitive the clutch-accelerator coordination was and how he needed to keep the engine revving to avoid stalling.

"Fred's very particular. You have to know certain things."

"Fred and I have an understanding. I'll pick you up at five-thirty."

He left her outside the dentist's watching anxiously as he drove sedately away. Fred's engine needed a bit of maintenance. He'd done that as soon as he'd arrived back at the blue house. There wasn't much he didn't know about engines, and Fred's was basic in the extreme. Whoever did the regular service should be strung up. A rip-off merchant taking advantage of Phoebe's lack of knowledge. Fred purred with delight when they went for a test spin to beachside Dalmeny for a swim before lunch—lunch being a proper old-fashioned Aussie burger with everything from the local takeaway, eaten overlooking the beach and washed down with a large chilled green tea.

In the afternoon he investigated the corrugated iron shed in the back garden more thoroughly than he had the day before. He'd had only a cursory look then. After a morning trip to the large supermarket in the shopping plaza, Phoebe had wanted to spend the rest of Monday on the beach. Fair enough. It was her holiday weekend before she started the new job, and he was more than happy to swim and laze in the sun, keeping her company. He was her guest.

And she was good company—undemanding, extremely attractive and relaxing to be with now that the wedding was behind them and the relationship had been sorted into the just-friends category. He'd still kiss her given half a chance and a modicum of encouragement, but she kept her distance. *Okay.*

Inside, the shed was even more ovenlike than outside. He propped the door open and waited a few minutes for trapped heat to escape.

A shriek of rage erupted from next door. *Kids.* Little ones who fought a lot. He shook his head and shuddered as two more voices joined in, one wailing and the other, the mother's, saying, "If you do that again, Timmy, I'll lock your bike away in the shed."

"Timmy rode on my foot," screamed the wailing one.

Parenthood. You'd have to be insane. Brady grimaced and stuck his head through the shed doorway. A slight breeze had helped things along, but he was dripping sweat within minutes of stepping inside.

Phoebe's gran's things had overflowed from the house to here.

Several ancient suitcases were stacked on the workbench along with two broken kitchen chairs and a folding card table. Gardening tools were propped haphazardly in one corner; an old Victa lawn mower had seen better days but must still work, judging by the grass clippings stuck on the wheels. Her grass could do with a trim, one morning before the day heated up.

On the shelves along one wall he poked into various tins and old plastic ice cream tubs and found nails, screws, nuts, bolts, tap washers . . . The laundry tap dripped. He'd fix that too and check the other taps. She had three hammers of varying sizes, all rusted and unused for decades; two chisels and a few screwdrivers; a hacksaw with a broken blade; a fairly new stepladder; worn gardening gloves he'd be reluctant to stick his hands into; two mousetraps; two paint brushes so stiff he couldn't bend the bristles; a half-full bottle of turps; snail bait pellets; a horseshoe; a pair of Dutch wooden clogs; rose fertilizer; a wheelbarrow; a red-striped deck chair. No sandpaper.

He could pick some up at the plaza on his way to collect Phoebe. He checked his watch. That gave him just over two hours. He'd fix the drip.

She was waiting on the footpath where he'd left her when he met her at twenty to six. He stopped a few steps from where she stood. She was still wearing the anxious expression, still very pretty. The sight of her made him smile with a spontaneous rush of delight. She opened the door and climbed in.

"Hello. Good day?" he asked.

No answering smile. "Hi. Yes. You're late. I thought you'd had an accident."

"Nope. Sorry. I got held up at the supermarket. I had a really good day." He peered over his shoulder and whipped smartly into the line of cars.

"Fred go okay?"

"Fred's going beautifully. I can see why you love driving him. He's fun." He was a bit cramped, but it was better driving than being the passenger. He glanced at her for a reaction.

Her head was cocked to one side as she listened, brow creased. She gave him an accusing frown. "He sounds different."

"I gave him a tune-up. He doesn't stall now."

"*You* did?" Accusation turned to horror.

"Yep. I don't think your mechanic is any good."

Horror turned to indignation. "John next door does it for me. Mate's rates."

"Is he a mechanic?"

"No. He just knows about engines."

"Doesn't know much."

"He's nice and he helps me a lot." Indignation retreated to stubborn defense. It was time to back off.

"I'm sure he does." If nice John was the one giving expert advice on the guttering, no doubt a second opinion was in order. And just how nice was John? What was his real motive for helping out Phoebe? He was certainly free with his advice and inept mechanical assistance. On which side did he live? Was he the guy with the kids?

Brady opened his mouth to ask, but she said, "Are you having dinner at my place tonight?"

He looked across at her, surprised, mouth still open. Why wouldn't he eat with her that night? "I'd planned to. Is that all right?"

"Sure, yes. I just thought you might have moved, that's all."

"Moved?" The Ocean View was expecting him the next day; he'd checked.

"To the motel."

The motel! Lindy had booked one night in some cheapo place. He remembered now. Phoebe sounded as though she'd been hanging out waiting for him to go, expecting him to have already exited her life when he'd been doing the exact opposite: settling in, unexpectedly enjoying himself.

"Okay. I thought I'd go after dinner. I'm cooking tonight. Can't ignore all the fresh seafood around here. I'm making paella taught to me by a Spanish lady called Viviane." Thank goodness he'd bought a French-style fruit flan from a bakery for dessert. What was that motel called? He had no idea. "A special farewell meal," he added.

"You'd forgotten, hadn't you?"

He flung her a quick glance as they rounded the corner to her street. Her face would split if she grinned any wider.

"No."

"You had so. What's the name of the motel?"

He swung into the driveway and roared into the garage, turned the engine off and handed her the keys. Her eyes were alight with laughter; she looked as though she'd burst any minute. She was a hard girl to impress. If she wasn't annoyed with him, she was laughing at him.

"Haven't a clue."

She laughed so much she dropped the keys on the floor.

"Do you?" he asked, when she'd fumbled around and found them under her feet. If she didn't know the name of the place, he was out of luck.

"No." She almost fell out the door she was so weak with laughing. It wasn't that funny.

"Have you been at the laughing gas? I didn't know dentists still used it."

Her arms wrapped across her stomach; she leaned on the car and gasped. "You should see your face. So . . . so . . . serious. Pretending you hadn't forgotten . . . when you had . . ." She drew in a deep breath and wiped her streaming eyes.

He raised his voice over her cackling. "Think we should ring Lindy and ask?"

Another explosive burst of mirth. "On their honeymoon? She'd love that. To be reminded of us."

"Good point." *Us.* It sounded nice despite the irritating and humiliating accompaniment of laughter. "What do you suggest?" He leaned into the rear of Fred and grasped the grocery bags, trying to ignore the giggles. It was hopeless.

"Ruth might know." She was under control a bit now. Thank goodness. He followed her to the house. The next-door neighbors were having a barbecue. Peace had broken out. Childish laughter wafted over the fence along with the smell of frying onion and sausages. Dad was home, maintaining order.

Ruth didn't know. Phoebe came into the kitchen, where Brady was peeling prawns.

"They have no idea."

"How many motels are there? I suppose I could ring around."

"If you like. There are lots. Alternatively, you could stay here and just not turn up wherever it is."

"Pretty poor form."

"Yes." She walked out and came back with the phone book. "There are fifteen motels, three hotels, plus B and Bs. I'll read out names and see if any ring a bell." She reached the end. "Nothing sounds familiar."

"No. I'll have to call them all." *Bummer.* Phoebe didn't seem fussed one way or the other. He'd much rather stay, but he wouldn't like to mess the motel people around. He'd had enough of that behavior from his own clients, thoughtless rich idiots changing their plans at the last minute and forgetting or not bothering to call with advance warning. "I'll get the seafood ready first."

"I'll change, then make a start for you. Did you get dessert?"

"Secret."

She smiled, tilted her head, raised her eyebrows, and left the kitchen. She couldn't wait to get rid of him. In fact, she was going to make quite sure he did move out that night. He firmed his mouth. *Fine.* He'd done his best to make sure he was a help in the house, tuned up her car, fixed the dripping taps—three as it turned out—and cooked dinner. He could do no more. She didn't want him to stay.

He found the largest pan she had. The shower started. Would she notice the new, improved taps? Probably not.

She'd left the phone book open on the bench. He pulled out his phone and called the last name on the list. Lindy had said it was a cheap place. He'd start at the bottom and work up. He rang three places before Phoebe reappeared, fragrant and fresh in a white T-shirt and shorts, hair wispy and damp around her smooth neck.

"Any luck?"

"No." He dialed the next.

"Crest Motel," said a voice in his ear.

"Hello. Do you have a booking in the name of Winters for tonight?" They would; he remembered the name now.

"You should stay here tonight."

"One moment, please."

Had he heard Phoebe right? Brady put his hand over the phone. "What?"

"Cancel it," she hissed. "Silly to move twice. And I don't feel like driving you anywhere this evening. I'm tired. "

"Hello. Yes, we have a Brady Winters for one night."

"I'm sorry, but I'm going to have to cancel my booking."

"No problem. Thank you for letting us know."

"Will there be a cancellation fee?"

"No charge."

"Really? Thank you very much. Good night." Brady disconnected. Had she meant it? Holding her gaze, he said, "Are you sure?"

She turned away, carelessly breaking the contact. "Too late now. It's only one extra night. And it's true, I'm tired."

He stuck the phone into his pocket and turned back to the dinner preparations. Onion and garlic. Peel and chop. "Too many teeth wear you out?"

"Too much concentrating after a holiday and a lot of standing."

"Did you enjoy it?"

Phoebe filled a glass with chilled water from the fridge. "Yes, but I'm not sure about long-term."

How weak-willed she was, suggesting he stay that night. *Pathetic.* Who was she kidding, thinking she could resist him? She loved having him in her home, loved spending yesterday doing mundane things. Loved it—to the point where she could quite easily ask him to stay for the remaining weeks. But she wouldn't. That would be a massive mistake leading to complete devastation when he left—which he would, without a backward glance, after his last appointment.

"If you want to stay living here, there's not a lot of choice," he said.

There he went again, rubbing it in about small-town life, proving her point. The last thing Brady Winters would do was live in Narooma, and he certainly wouldn't for the sake of a woman.

"I meant for the rest of my life," she said.

"So did I."

She drained the glass and thumped it down on the bench. "Need any help?"

He shook his head. "No, thanks."

That was lucky. She didn't want to help, didn't want to stand next to him torturing herself by wondering if he wanted to kiss her again. Or she might freak them both out and kiss him. "I have to prepare for those weddings."

Phoebe sat on her bed with her laptop open before her. Wedding number one, eleven A.M. in Tilba, was ready. Number two, at one o'clock at the golf club, was almost ready, and number three, at five-fifteen at a private house in Dalmeny, wasn't ready at all. The couple were very slow to respond to her queries despite booking her only two weeks earlier and sounding delighted she was available. It was very unusual for an excited bride and groom to be so slack with arrangements. She had some information but not enough to do more than a workmanlike service, and that was not her style at all. Personal was her trademark and why people called her, specifically, for their big day.

She fired off another e-mail to the girl in question. If she didn't hear by the next day, she'd phone—again. They still hadn't confirmed the rehearsal on Thursday. Not much more she could do about that one. Brady sure had a point about letting people know. It was straight-out courtesy. Just because she was being paid didn't make her some sort of switch-on, switch-off commodity.

Delicious aromas wafted in from the kitchen. Paella. She'd never eaten paella. Who was the Spanish lady who cooked and taught Brady? Another Juanita? Brady wouldn't have married anyone on impulse or otherwise; that was for sure. She sniffed, eyes closed. Delicious. Onions, garlic, spices . . . "Paella," she murmured, savoring the *l*'s and allowing the *a* to float. How exotic-sounding that was. "Paella."

Next morning, Brady dropped her at work again.

"I'll pick you up at five-thirty," he said as she collected her purse and opened the door.

"Thanks."

She hesitated. Her smile was a tad uncertain, and she looked about ready to say something she didn't want to and he wouldn't want to hear. He should make it easy for her. The last thing he wished to do was impose himself where he wasn't welcome. Had he done that already?

"What's wrong?"

"Nothing. Don't crash my car." The smile widened to a grin.

That wasn't what she was worried about, but she wasn't going to spit it out. "I won't. I'll make a start on the windows today. After lunch, I'll move out so by the time you come home, you'll have the house to yourself again. Back to normal."

"Not quite," she murmured. She opened the door, but he whipped out his hand and held her arm.

"What's wrong, Phoebe? Don't you want me to work on the house? Is that it? Is it the money thing? Because if it is, you don't have to worry. I'm more than happy to do it, and you're lending me the car in exchange, which I really appreciate."

A tiny frown marred her perfect brow under the wisps of copper-and-molasses hair. Her perfume wafted into his nostrils and teased his brain. She always smelled delicious. "No, it's not that. . . ." She bit her lower lip gently. "It's nothing." She gave him another smile. "Don't be late this time."

"Promise I won't."

He waved and headed into Narooma rush-hour traffic. Rush ten-minute traffic. He grinned to himself. He'd swing by the paint shop first and pick up some color samples, and he'd need putty and Poly-filla.

The harbor sparkled in the morning sun. The water on this stretch of coast was an extraordinary color, greeny-blue crystal. A couple of motorized game-fishing cruisers were chugging along the channel, which snaked between man-made breakwaters, heading for the narrow exit to the open sea. Six or seven more were already out bobbing on the vast blue Pacific.

A sudden urge to set foot on a boat flooded his system, and he swung Fred toward the historic Town Wharf. He parked and walked across the narrow street, over a walkway, and to the long wharf running parallel to the shore, relishing the wooden planks beneath his feet and the slosh of waves against the barnacle-encrusted pylons. Seagulls wheeled and squawked overhead. It was so familiar, the smell of the sea, bilge water, diesel exhaust, fish, all mixing and fermenting to a ripe brew in the heat.

He paused by the big blue notice of the Blue Seas Cruise Company attached to the railing, reading their cruise times and charges. A half-day trip to Montague Island. That'd be interesting on several levels. His yearning to set foot on a deck would be assuaged; he'd visit the island, which was a national park reserve; he'd see how this little company operated. They offered dive trips too. *Excellent.* He could hire gear.

If no tour boats were in, which they weren't, tickets were available from the tourist information center. Would Phoebe enjoy an evening cruise? He'd bet she'd never gone on one of the tourist excursions. Locals rarely did unless they had visitors to entertain.

Half an hour later, he climbed into Fred with tickets and brochures in his pocket. Half-day cruise to the island on Thursday morning. Evening cruise with Phoebe on Saturday, and he'd take her to a late dinner at the golf club afterward. Dive trip to swim with fur seals and explore the wreck of the *Lady Darling* the following week.

Now to work.

Twenty minutes later, he attacked the west-facing window frames, armed with a ladder, sandpaper, and elbow grease and wearing a wide-brimmed straw hat he'd found in the laundry. Those kids next door were at it again, screaming and yelling one minute, laughing the next. The mother was in charge that day. Dad must be at work. From the ladder he could see over the fence into their yard. The two little boys were playing on the swing set. Mum pegged washing on the line and refereed the battlefield. She gave him a cursory glance and continued with her task.

"G'day, mate," said a male voice from ground level. Brady looked down on a white toweling hat above a bulging beer belly.

"Hello."

"You're doing some work for Phoebe, I see."

"Yes." He climbed down and extended his hand. "Brady Winters."

The retiree had a neat gray goatee and a pair of skinny legs with knobby brown knees that emerged from khaki shorts and ended in flip-flops. He gave Brady's hand a good solid shake.

"John Hyslop. Live next door. The wife and I retired down here from Sydney eight years ago."

"It's a nice place to retire to."

"Best place in the world. You can keep your Rivieras and tropical islands. Nothing beats the South Coast of New South Wales." A pair of false teeth gleamed in the bright morning sunlight. "You're new in town, aren't you? Haven't seen you around." Pale blue eyes studied Brady with interest. "Staying long?"

"About two weeks. I'm helping Phoebe out while I'm here. Doing a few odd jobs."

The solution to the mystery of his sudden appearance dawned. "Were you here for that wedding? It was her best friend getting married."

"Yes." Lindy didn't seem to be Phoebe's best friend. She certainly wasn't now.

"Strange she never mentioned you to us." He took another gimlet-eyed survey of his person. "We keep an eye on her, Margaret and I. Girl living on her own, you know? Needs a man to give her a hand occasionally."

"That's very kind."

"It's neighborly, that's what it is. We do that in these small communities. Something city folk could do with more of." He glared at Brady accusingly. "Where are you from?"

"Melbourne originally but I've been working in France for the last few years."

That news surprised the suspicion from his face. "France? The wife and I went there on a tour two years ago. Saw the lot, Paris, Nice, the wine regions, the battlefields of the First and Second World Wars . . . Marvelous trip. I suppose you *parlez vous français,* do you? Never could get my tongue around it. English will do me, has done for seventy-one years."

"Yes. I speak French. I have to, because I work there."

"What do you do?"

"I work on a yacht. Charter cruises."

"Oho. Sailing rich sods round the Mediterranean, eh?"

"Something like that." Brady put one foot on the ladder as a hint.

"Those people Phoebe rented the house to were a noisy crowd. Hope she doesn't do that again. I've been meaning to pop over and tell her. Played their music late at night, really loudly. Woke the wife up."

"I'll let her know, but I don't think she'll be doing it again."

"I told her I didn't think it was a good idea, but between you and me, she needs the money." He eyed the sandpaper in Brady's hand. "I hope you're not overcharging her. I could've done any little jobs. All she needed to do was ask."

"I'm not charging her anything. I'm doing it as a friend in exchange for the use of her car while I'm here." Painting the house was hardly a little job.

"Do you know what you're doing?"

Brady swallowed a retort he'd regret. "Yes I do, as a matter of fact."

John harrumphed and coughed to cover it up. "Well, if you need a hand, give me a shout. I'm right next door. That side." He jerked his thumb toward the far side of the house.

"Will do, thanks." Brady climbed up and began scraping again. Flakes of blue paint fluttered about in the hot air. John stood watching.

"How long have you known Phoebe?" he asked after a few minutes of silence, during which Brady hoped he'd leave.

"About a week. Just over, actually."

"A week! You're a fast worker."

Brady stopped and stared down at the rapidly-becoming-annoying man at knee level. "What do you mean by that?" Flakes of old paint had lodged in his hat.

John rapidly and correctly assessed his irritation level and backpedaled. "Nothing, nothing. Phoebe doesn't have many male visitors. . . ." He gulped and tried again. "I mean, Phoebe doesn't . . . have people to stay very often. Ever. Certainly not men."

"I'm not staying here. I'm staying up the road at the Ocean View." *Phoebe doesn't have male visitors. No boyfriends? None that this old codger knows about, anyway.* The thought was surprisingly pleasing. Other men pawing at his girl, his friend, was a repugnant idea. Kissing her the way he had. Phoebe responding the way she had . . . John interrupted the increasingly uncomfortable sequence of thought.

"Oh, right. Of course. I didn't mean to insinuate anything . . . untoward."

"Of course not."

"No. She's a lovely girl."

"She is." *A truly lovely girl. Special and wonderful in so many ways.*

"Well, I'd better leave you to it. The wife will be after me for wasting time. I'm supposed to be trimming the herbaceous borders."

"See you later, John."

"Bye. Pop over for a cuppa sometime. Meet Margaret. She makes a mean scone. Homemade strawberry jam too."

"Thanks." Brady returned to his sanding with increased fervor. *Meet Margaret? Drink tea and politely undergo another third degree? Not likely.* How did Phoebe stand having these people breathing down her neck and examining every move she made, assessing every visitor she had? Robyn in the store was bad enough; these neighbors were even worse. They were closer and felt they had the right to interfere, as if age gave them that license.

"Who are you?" A piping little voice jolted him from his caustic reverie. It was the kid from next door. Was there no end to these sticky beaks? And this one looked to be about four—in training early.

"I'm Brady. Who are you?"

"Timmy. I've got a truck." He held up a yellow dump truck covered in sand. "It's yellow."

"It's very nice."

"What are you doing to Phoebe's house?"

"I'm going to paint the window frames."

"Why are you rubbing them?"

"I have to take the old paint off first."

"Why?"

"So the new paint stays on better."

"What color?"

"Blue."

"It's already blue."

"This will be a bit darker blue."

"Are you Phoebe's friend?"

"Yes."

He giggled. "You're her boyfriend. I need to do a wee wee."

"Okay." He was saved. How would he have answered that one? Brady smiled as the little figure scampered across the yard toward the house but stopped suddenly and dropped his shorts.

A yell came from the back door. "Timothy, how many times have I told you to come inside to do a wee?"

"I tried but I couldn't wait."

He finished the windows on both sides by lunchtime. They had been the worst. The front and back were sheltered by the verandahs and needed only light work, although the putty was crumbling away all round the glass. John was right about the eaves; they were rotten in places. Lots of places. He'd clear the gutters for her so at least the next time it rained, the water could try to escape. It might be better to remove them completely.

As he sat out in front with a sandwich and iced tea, admiring the ocean view, a phrase he'd seen plastered across a FOR SALE sign on a similar old cottage on his way to Dalmeny sprang to mind: *Renovate or detonate*. That was really the solution here. He'd choose detonate if it were his decision. The block was worth ten times more than the house. Gran had chosen well all those years ago, despite being a crabby old bird by all accounts.

A two-story place, like the group house they'd shared the past week, would be the way to go. Big open-plan living space incorporating the kitchen, dining room, and lounge so all the areas took advantage of the view—a view that was even more spectacular here, especially up a level. The house would need to be turned slightly on the block to take in the full 180-degree coastline north and south and skim the treetops across the road.

He drained his glass and stood up. Idle speculation. Daydreams. He had the money but not the property. Phoebe had the property but not the money. Neither had the inclination. She'd blow a gasket if he suggested knocking the place down.

Chapter Ten

"Don't forget. Your appointment is at ten-thirty." Phoebe waved to Brady and closed the door. Fred whizzed away. Brady had done a good job on the engine. Fred hadn't sounded so happy in years. She turned and entered the office.

Brady would be gone in a couple of weeks. In a matter of days he had become a fixture in her life, dropping her off and picking her up, preparing dinner, working on the house, nailing palings back on the fence. He even mowed the lawn, wrestling with the Beast and taming both it and her enthusiastic grass. She hated the heavy old mower, but his comment was that it must be the noisiest thing he'd heard in his life and that he'd cleaned the engine.

His living up the road at the Ocean View made no difference at all. He spent 90 percent of his time at her house and appeared very happy there. Thank goodness she had this job to go to, or through unrelenting exposure, she'd fall totally in love with him and forget that he was just filling in time till he could leave, keeping himself from the perils of boredom with handyman antics. Not contemplating a change of lifestyle and a return to Australia. Nothing like that. *Remember. Friends.*

"Morning, Phoebe." Felicity smiled at her from behind the reception desk.

"Morning."

"Is your friend brave enough to come in today?"

"I think so."

"He looked petrified last week."

"I know. He didn't want to come at all. Thought the tooth might get better on its own."

"As if. By the way, we can fit him in on Tuesday next week as well as Friday and cancel his last appointment on the following Wednesday. Lucky for him Mrs. Forbes has had to go into hospital. But not for her," she added hastily. "He'll be able to head home sooner. He seemed anxious to get away when he made the appointments. In fact, he was really annoyed at having to stick around so long. Can't blame him, really."

"I know." What would he say when Felicity made the offer?

Phoebe went into the little staff room and stowed her bag away. An ache started up in her stomach. A voice wailed in her head. She didn't want him to go. This was exactly what she knew would happen. It was inevitable, regardless of how she kidded herself that she could ignore him and resist him and keep the attraction at bay. It was impossible. And he made it a billion times worse by being so nice! It was better the past week, when he was being obnoxious about the wedding and her views on family. Then at least she'd had something to focus on other than how sexy he was.

One more week. He hadn't mentioned leaving.

He came in on time, smiling. He was a different man from the nervous wreck of the past Friday.

"Good morning," said Graeme. "How's the tooth holding up?"

"Fine. It was a bit sore for a couple of days, but I don't have any pain now. I'm careful how I eat, though."

"Good, good. We'll do that crown today."

Brady smiled at Phoebe as he sat down. She slipped the bib around his neck and withdrew from his line of sight. Graeme adjusted the chair, switched on the light, and leaned over, brandishing one of his shiny silver implements. "Let's have a look, then, shall we?"

Phil rang just after lunch, inviting Brady to play golf on Sunday afternoon.

"Great. I'd love to. I haven't had a chance to get out there yet."

"What have you been doing?"

"Painting Phoebe's window frames. I'll finish today. Plus I've mown her lawn, fixed some taps, serviced the Beetle, and taken a trip to Montague Island. That was great."

"Goodness. We thought you'd be having a holiday. How's the tooth?"

"Jaw's numb but it's all fixed. I have to go back next week for some other stuff. Two appointments, then I'm done."

"When are you leaving?"

"I'm not sure. I haven't rung the airline yet about flights. I suppose I could leave next weekend."

"Why don't we have dinner on Sunday night at the club after golf? Ruth and Phoebe can join us."

"Good idea."

"Right. See you at two on Sunday."

"Thanks."

He went back to the last window. Two coats all round, and they were looking good. Phoebe was delighted. Surprising and pleasing her was fun. She'd enjoy dinner with Ruth and Phil. And he was yet to spring the surprise cruise the next evening. He might have to find somewhere else for dinner rather than go to the golf club on consecutive nights. That winery was good but too far out of town after a cruise. Maybe a quiet night in instead with some sort of takeaway. Thai or Chinese.

Leave?

He whacked the lid back onto the paint tin. She'd have a bit left for touch-ups. He'd be back on board *Lady Lydia* in a fortnight. He'd have to catch up with her in Athens. It'd be chilly. It was still winter. Hard to imagine being cold, in this heat. Michel had said they'd hit some freezing gale-force winds when they left Marseilles.

Brady carried the paint to the shed, then set about cleaning the brush and his hands. What was next on the agenda? He had another week to fill. Golf on Sunday. Diving on Thursday. Dentist on Tuesday and Friday, but that wouldn't take long, Tucker said. Maybe another round with Phil?

It was a pity Phoebe had to work. They'd have the day together tomorrow, though, and half of Sunday and the next weekend. He'd try to get a flight out on Monday so he could spend that weekend with her as well. He stopped mid-scrub, blue soap froth up his arms. Why was he arranging his travel around Phoebe? Since when did a woman dictate what he did?

He frowned and plunged his hands back into the sink as the realization struck hard: she wasn't dictating anything. Quite the opposite. She'd been relieved when he moved up the road to the Ocean View. He was justifying and organizing himself to spend as much time as possible with her before he left. Why? Answer: she was an attractive girl. But so were all the others he'd flirted with and dated over the years. He'd never had a problem leaving any of them before.

Phoebe gave no indication of wanting him to stay. She was more concerned with the deal they'd struck over the painting, but was reconciled and happy now with what he was doing. Why was the thought of leaving her physically painful? He snorted in disgust. *Stupid idiot. Don't get suckered in any deeper.* He rinsed his arms and grabbed the towel. As soon as he was on board *Lady Lydia,* life would regain its normality. Brady Winters would be back on an even keel, sailing the seven seas with no ties to bind him.

Another thought hit him like a bucket load of dead fish: what if he'd been imposing all week, making the assumption she was happy to have him prepare dinner and eat with her every night when in reality she might be gritting her teeth and wishing he'd leave her alone? But she'd say so. Wouldn't she? Or was she too polite and kind?

Bad signs, these thoughts. He was fast becoming involved and entangled. It was time to backpedal and make his escape.

He rang the airline. He could take a late Saturday afternoon flight from Sydney to Athens via Melbourne and London—another tortuous marathon of travel. He'd have to leave Narooma either very early on Saturday—way too early—or Friday afternoon. That'd work. His last appointment with Tucker was at nine.

He booked the flights plus a room at an airport hotel in Sydney. *Done.* Decision made.

There she was in her usual spot, looking anxiously for him to appear. He double-parked, ignoring the horn-tooting driver behind, and she ran across and jumped in beside him.

"Hi." Her smile gave him goose bumps. It was the happy one. The tension had completely gone from her face.

"Hi." He slid into the traffic. "Phoebe, I was wondering . . ."

"Yes?"

"Would you rather be alone tonight? . . . I mean, are you sick of having me around all the time . . . eating at your place every night . . ."

"Are you sick of cooking?" The look she gave him was one of pure horrified surprise. "I'm sorry . . . I just assumed . . . you know . . . You should have said . . ."

"No! Not at all. It's the least I could do. You've been so kind to me, lending me Fred all week. I thought you might like some space, that's all."

"Oh, I see. Thanks . . ." Shocked embarrassment gave way to relief.

Make it easy for her. "Actually, I've got something tonight I'd—"

She jumped in. "That's fine. Don't feel you have to stay with me. I'm sure you'd rather be out somewhere else for a change."

No, he wouldn't, but the way she leaped on the suggestion was enough of a hint. TV in his room with a pizza tonight.

"Oh. I'm playing golf with Phil on Sunday afternoon, and he suggested we meet him and Ruth for dinner at the golf club afterwards."

"That'll be lovely."

"I doubt whether my game will be. I haven't played for ages."

"I've never played golf. Never been the slightest bit interested."

"What a waste, living where you do."

She laughed. She sounded happy, carefree, and to his ear relieved not to be stuck with him again. He didn't go into the house with her when he'd parked Fred in the garage. He handed her the keys. "I finished the windows today."

"It looks fantastic. I don't know how to thank you." Her smile was more than enough reward.

"No problem. You already have. Well. I'd better be off."

He took a few steps along the driveway toward his self-imposed lonely evening. He hadn't told her he'd booked to leave.

"Brady, are you coming to the wedding with me tomorrow?" *Wedding? What wedding?* "In Tilba. Remember you said you'd like to come because you'd be stir-crazy by now? But you've been so busy maybe you'd rather not." Her expression gave no indication of how he should respond, but any time in her company was a bonus.

"Of course. What time?" Vague memories stirred. It seemed a long time since the past weekend. Hadn't she mentioned other weddings?

Her eyes narrowed at his ready reply, but she said, "I have to leave about twenty past ten."

"Okay. I'll be here. How many are you doing tomorrow, did you say?" *What about his surprise, the evening cruise?* Thank goodness he'd kept it to himself, or he'd look like a complete fool. If the timing was wrong, he could cancel his booking and she'd never know a thing.

"Three."

"When will you be home?"

"About six. Why?"

They'd just scrape it in. He grinned. "I have a surprise planned."

Her eyes sparkled. "Tell me."

He had an almost irresistible urge to kiss her. "No. Just make sure you get home by six. See you tomorrow." He turned and sauntered away, glad she couldn't see the ridiculous, uncontrollable grin plastered across his face.

The wedding was in a house a little way out of the village of Central Tilba, but Phoebe dropped Brady in the main street, which was awash with visitors. He found a coffee shop and ordered breakfast, sitting under a shade umbrella on the terrace at the rear of the cream-and-rusty-red-painted wooden building with a view of rolling green hills and valleys. The landscape was quite beautiful and very lush. It was dairy country, thus the cheese Phoebe had mentioned. He'd buy some for Phoebe at one of the arty little shops.

The plastic-covered place mat on his table said *Tilba* was an aboriginal word for *wind*. That must mean the neighboring tiny village of Tilba Tilba was a windy, windy place. Central Tilba and Tilba Tilba had a combined population of less than a hundred. The teenage waitress deposited his coffee and a plate of eggs and bacon on the place mat.

"Is there another Tilba somewhere?" he asked.

"Tilba Tilba is a couple of kilometers south."

"But you can't be Central Tilba with only two towns. You need three at least." He smiled at her frown. "Shouldn't there be another Tilba? To the north?"

She backed away. "I don't know. There are only two that I know of."

"Thanks." So much for facetious chitchat. He attacked his breakfast.

Moments later someone blocked the sun. "Brady? Brady Winters? Is it? It is!"

He looked up at the figures silhouetted against the glare. A man and a woman stared down at him, the man with a beaming smile carving his face into two half-moons. He was completely bald, or at least shaven headed, and very rotund. Vaguely familiar. The voice. The slim brown-haired woman wasn't; she was smiling politely.

"Jeff," his assailant cried. "Jeff Rogers. From Moonee Street."

Moonee Street. Round the corner from where he lived in high school. He and Jeff had caught the same bus every day for years.

"Jeff. Mate!" He stood up and grasped the outstretched hand. "How are you?"

"Fine. Doing well. This is Janette, my wife. Brady and I went to high school together."

"Hello." Janette gave his hand a dainty shake.

"What are you doing these days?" asked Brady.

"I'm a pharmacist in Narooma. You?"

"I'm based in France. I own a charter yacht."

"Really? Good for you. You always liked the sea, didn't you?" He chortled with delight. Brady remembered that laugh. Jeff had always been a happy boy, an eternal optimist.

"Would you like to join me?" Brady indicated the spare seats at his table.

Jeff glanced at Janette and she nodded.

"So what brings you to Tilba?" she asked, when they'd settled down opposite him and the waitress had taken their order for tea and scones.

"I'm here with a friend. She's celebrant at a wedding. She's from Narooma too, but I came to be best man at Alex Moore's wedding last week. Remember him, Jeff?"

"Sure do. And Dave. You three were inseparable."

"Yes. He was best man as well. We don't get together much anymore. Last time was at Dave's wedding three years ago."

"Are you married?" Janette asked.

Brady shook his head. He sipped his cooling coffee. What was it with women? Why did they always want to establish marital status?

"Brady won't ever get married. He always said that."

"When he was at high school." Janette snorted with disdain. "Give him some credit, love. He's grown up since then. He can change his mind."

"If I find the right girl, I'll consider it. Haven't found her yet." Had he? His argument was on shaky ground when he looked at Phoebe. But that would be put right the next week when he was back at sea.

"I found the right girl," Jeff said. "Then I went and married Janette."

"Idiot." She punched his arm affectionately as he guffawed at his joke. "And now you're stuck with me."

Jeff kissed her cheek. "Best move I ever made. Laid eyes on you and it was all over, Red Rover. How much longer are you staying, Brady? If you've got time, you must come for dinner."

"I'll be here another week. That would be great. Thank you."

"And bring your friend. Do you play golf?"

"I do. I'm playing on Sunday with Alex's father-in-law." Would Phoebe want to come? He'd like it if she did.

"We should have a game. I go early—before work. Best time of the day in summer."

"I agree. You're on, Jeff. When?"

"How about Tuesday at five-thirty?"

"Done. How long have you been in Narooma?"

"Not long. We bought the pharmacy last year. Janette teaches at the primary school."

"Do you like it here?"

"We love it," he said. "We're still exploring the area, hence our trip to Tilba for morning tea."

"It's a nice little town."

"Heritage listed. They're keeping all these lovely old wooden buildings the way they were built."

Brady looked at his watch. "I'm sorry. I'll have to leave. Phoebe will be picking me up soon, and I want to have a look around first."

"Pop in to the Plaza Pharmacy and say hello on Monday. Otherwise I'll see you on Tuesday morning."

"Will do. Thanks. Nice to meet you, Janette."

Phoebe cruised slowly down the main street, which was really the only street in Central Tilba. Brady should be on the corner of the parking area. If he wasn't, it'd be a nuisance, because she'd have to park and wait, which would make her rush for the next wedding, back in Narooma. What was his surprise? She loved surprises. Nice ones, not the "Alex is married" type.

He stepped forward suddenly from behind a group of strolling tourists and waved. A brown paper carry bag dangled from his other hand. He must have been souvenir shopping.

"How did it go?" he asked when he jumped in beside her.

"Fine. How about you? Did you enjoy Central Tilba?"

"Yep. I bought you this." He displayed the carry bag. "Cheese and honey."

"Thanks. Is that the surprise?" The highway was fast approaching. She slowed Fred for the intersection.

"No." He gave a self-satisfied chuckle. "I got a surprise, though. I ran into a guy I went to school with. Jeff Rogers."

"The pharmacist?"

"Yes. Do you know him?"

"Only by name. He's new."

"He and his wife were here having morning tea. They invited us to dinner next week."

"That's nice." A gap opened up in the traffic, and she whipped onto the highway in front of someone towing a boat.

"You don't sound very enthusiastic." He sounded disappointed.

"Sorry."

"You don't have to go."

"I'll go." Might as well meet the Rogerses. Why not? They'd be here long after Brady had departed. So would she.

"Only if you want to."

For heaven's sake. Why make such a fuss? "I'll go." She forced a grin. "I never knock back a free feed. When is it?"

He returned the smile. "I don't know yet. We're playing golf early on Tuesday. He'll tell me then."

He'd still made no mention of leaving. He must have organized his flights by now. How could he not say? She gritted her teeth. A lorry loaded with gigantic logs roared past in the next lane, rocking Fred with its slipstream. Those truckies drove like lunatics. He'd be crawling up the next hill. She accelerated round a car and caravan.

"Slow down. You'll make it in time."

Poor Fred was screaming like a jet. She eased her foot off the accelerator, and the whine decreased in volume.

"Calm down." Brady was leaning against the door, smiling at her from behind his dark glasses, cool as could be. Couldn't he tell she was going to miss him more than she'd ever missed anything or anyone in the world? Didn't he realize that every sweet thing he did, every careless little gesture of kindness, like the gift of honey and cheese, was pure torture? How was she supposed to go out to dinner with him to the home of those friends of his, invited like a couple but acting as friends? How? They'd spot how she felt in an instant. And being old friends, they would know immediately that Brady Casanova had made another conquest. They'd add her to the mental list of his exes.

"Have you booked your flights?"

"Yep. Did it yesterday." He switched the radio on. An ad for mattresses came blasting out. He switched it off.

"And?" Was this denseness deliberate?

"I'm leaving Friday, flying out of Sydney on Saturday."

"Friday." *So soon.*

"Yes, it was either then or wait till the following Wednesday." He said this very casually, as if the information meant nothing to him and would mean even less to her.

"You couldn't do that."

"No. I have to get back. I'll have been away three weeks instead of one."

"I guess you're looking forward to getting home."

"I miss the *Lady Lydia,* that's for sure. But I'm not looking forward to the weather over there. Not after this great summer heat."

"Are you going to France?"

"No. Athens. She'll be there soon. We're taking someone around the islands."

"Wow. It sounds so exotic." Why would he want to stay a minute longer here than he had to? No reason at all.

He laughed. "I said you could come and crew."

"And I said I couldn't. Even before I had my job." Trail after him like a lovesick puppy? She had too much self-respect. What would his crew think? "I get seasick, remember?"

"Seasick? That's true, you did tell me that."

He lapsed into silence, staring out the window. Already in Greece onboard the boat. Not here anymore. Gone from her.

Phoebe arrived home from the third wedding at five past six in a foul mood. The whole thing had been a mess from start to finish, just as she'd feared when they'd canceled the rehearsal—something she'd discovered when she'd finally contacted the bride's mother, who laughed and said, "Oh, didn't Sharon tell you? We decided we didn't need a practice."

Despite dressing in the house, the bride was late. The groom mumbled and had to be prompted several times, the bride kept giggling and glancing at her bridesmaids, no one had thought to provide music, the photographer was someone's fourteen-year-old nephew, and the best man couldn't find the ring—not as a joke but really couldn't find it. A guest eventually picked it up off the grass. Hopeless! Some people would be hard-pressed to organize a trip to the shops, let alone a wedding.

But it was over and they were married. Thank goodness. What an exhausting day. With any luck Brady's surprise would be something restful she could enjoy with her feet up.

He was waiting on the front verandah and waved for her to stop in the driveway rather than put Fred away. That meant they were going out. She opened the door and he bounded forward. "You'd better change into jeans or something. And bring a jacket."

"Why?"

"You'll see."

"Is it tiring? I'm really not up for anything strenuous." But her residual annoyance was melting away under his eager smile. He was like a little kid with a secret, busting to tell but determined to keep the surprise.

"It's not strenuous, I promise. Just hurry."

Phoebe hesitated. "Brady, I . . ."

"Come on." He was so lovable. She was so weak in his presence. She couldn't refuse, couldn't disappoint him. She stirred her weary body and hurried.

"Brady took me on the evening cruise to the island yesterday as a surprise. It was fantastic." Staggering. A wonderful surprise. So much so, she'd kissed him. Only on the cheek, but it was something she'd vowed not to allow herself to do. He, fortunately, laughed it off as his due. Then he'd produced a motion sickness pill.

"How romantic." Ruth shared a glance with Phil, and they both smiled. He topped up their glasses.

"I only chose the evening cruise because Phoebe can't do the day one. I went last week during the day and it was great. I thought Phoebe would like it. Locals rarely do the tourist things." Brady stopped abruptly. "Have you?"

"We take guests out there sometimes. Or send them. We've been a few times. It is a fascinating trip." They were still casting secretive little smiling glances at each other. Why?

"Bit scary coming in and out through the entrance to the bar." Phoebe pulled her mouth down. "Didn't worry him, though." She smiled at Brady.

He'd been in his element, and loved it. She'd watched him standing in the bow, legs braced against the toss and pitch of the little boat as the incoming waves fought to prevent their exit through the narrow channel. And again as they rode in on the breakers, perilously close, in Phoebe's view, to smashing on the massive concrete blocks of the breakwater. He'd looked over his shoulder at her, gripping the edge of her seat with both hands, and laughed with pure joy. "It's great, isn't it?" he'd called, and she'd nodded. It was; the sunset was spectacular viewed from the ocean, and she hadn't felt the slightest bit seasick. And she'd been with him, sharing a little piece of his life, his passion.

"They do it every day. They know when the sea is up and it's too dangerous."

"Had you been out, Phoebe?" Phil asked.

"Yes, but only during the day. I've done a few weddings there."

"How lovely," said Ruth.

"One was. One was cold and drizzly, and the other the groom and half the guests got seasick on the way over."

"Did you?" asked Phil.

"No, I take a motion sickness pill before I go." She smiled at Brady. "He even remembered to give me one."

"Didn't want you throwing up and missing the sunset." How ridiculously pleased he was at how well his surprise had worked. Like a little boy. Or maybe he just liked going out on a boat after being land-bound for so long. "We come equipped with them for our guests until they get their sea legs."

"What about your boat, Brady?" asked Phil. "What's happening there?"

"I've been in touch regularly with Michel. He's my second in command. They can manage without me."

"But will you be in trouble for staying away from your job so long?" asked Ruth. "Will the company be angry?"

Brady laughed softly. He shook his head. "No. I'm the company."

"What do you mean?" Phoebe demanded over Ruth's gasp of astonishment.

He looked her in the eye. "It's my company. Only small as yet, but I own the *Lady Lydia*."

"You never said!" How could he keep a secret like that? Why would he keep a secret like that? "Do Alex and Dave know?"

"No. I don't think I mentioned it."

"You didn't think to mention it?" squeaked Phoebe. She met Ruth's equally flummoxed gaze. Here they were, thinking Brady was a footloose, carefree drifter with no ties, no prospects, and no ambition. It was an erroneous opinion that had colored their view—her view—from first meeting.

"How long have you owned it?" asked Phil eagerly.

"A bit over a year."

"How on earth did you come to . . . were you able to . . ." Phoebe stopped, groping for a tactful way to finish her question. Brady did it for her.

"How could I afford to buy a boat?"

She nodded. He clearly understood exactly what she was thinking. And he probably had a good idea all along what Lindy and the other girls thought of him too. He didn't set them straight. Why? Because he didn't care what anyone thought. Her included. He'd never cared right from when he was a boy finding his way alone.

"Exactly," said Ruth. "We always had the impression from what Alex told us that you were an itinerant crew member, but then he said just last week you were the skipper."

"I was itinerant until I met Wilhelm and Beate Burg. He's a very wealthy German businessman who loves sailing. I got a job crewing on their yacht one summer, and for some reason they took a liking to me. That was about eleven years ago now. They don't have children, so I became a sort of surrogate son to them."

So he did have a family. What was all that stuff about not caring about people? *Rubbish.*

"And they helped you?" Phil asked.

"Yes. Wilhelm gave me advice on investing and he helped me save enough to buy *Lady Lydia* and start my own company."

"How's it going?"

"Really well. I want to buy another boat next year."

How could they sit there calmly discussing boats when there was an elephant in the room?

"Why did you go on and on about not caring about having a family when all along these two German people were like parents to you?" The words burst out and brought the conversation to a screeching halt. Two male faces regarded her in wide-eyed astonishment.

"But they're not my family. I don't have a family. I said they regarded me as a *sort of* surrogate son, not that I regard them as my parents. Wilhelm and Beate help a lot of people gain their feet in business. I keep in touch with them, of course. We're very close."

"What wonderful people," said Ruth.

"They are."

"But why didn't you tell anyone? Why keep such a thing secret?"

Brady frowned. "It's not a secret. I just didn't think to say anything. The subject didn't come up."

"But it did. I asked you what you did on the boat on the very first day."

"And I told you. I'm the skipper."

"And you didn't think to expand on that to include the fact that you owned it?"

Brady shot a helpless glance at Phil. "No. You didn't ask."

Phil shrugged expressively. "Can't help you, mate."

"I'm sorry, Phoebe. I truly didn't think it was important. Skippering the *Lady Lydia* to me is the best thing in the world. That's what I love. Sailing. Forming my own company is a means to an end. I have to make a living somehow," he added. "And I don't want to be crewing for someone else the rest of my life."

Phoebe turned to Ruth. "What is it with these men? Is it me or them? None of them thought Alex's not telling Lindy about his Mexican marriage was an issue, and now Brady forgets to mention he owns a million-dollar yacht."

Ruth tilted her head. "I think men's brains are wired differently. Does it matter, Phoebe, that Brady didn't tell anyone?"

"I suppose not." Phoebe swallowed. Did it? No one else seemed to think so. "Maybe it *is* me."

Perhaps it didn't matter in the grand scheme of things, but it was hurtful; that's what it was. She'd thought they were friends, and real friends shared that type of information about themselves. He knew everything about her down to how she couldn't afford to fix the guttering on her house and what pajamas she wore.

It turned out she knew nothing about him, and he didn't want to enlighten her.

Chapter Eleven

Walking Phoebe home after dinner, Brady had the distinct feeling she was annoyed with him again. A half-moon didn't provide much light, and the isolated streetlights cast feeble pools of illumination every few hundred meters in her street. There was no footpath, but she strode down the middle of the quiet road beside him in the darkness, stiff and silent. His arm itched to slide around her shoulders.

Conversation during dessert and coffee had consisted mostly of Phil's and Ruth's asking about Europe and sailing the Med. Phoebe hardly said a word, all because he hadn't said he owned *Lady Lydia*. Where was his laughing, happy girl? How had he managed to upset her without even trying? He couldn't leave on Friday with this between them.

"I'm sorry I didn't tell you." Would stealing a kiss make things better or worse? "I thought we were friends."

He really wanted to kiss her. Denying himself over the past weeks had been torture. But that was how she wanted it.

"That's the trouble," she muttered.

He did hold her arm then, stopping her mid-stride and gently pulling her to face him. "What do you mean?" Did she want to be more than friends? Even as his heart jumped in his chest at the possibility, his brain overrode the delight with a cynical, habitual *Bit late for that now. She's wasted weeks.*

Her face shone pale in the dim light from the moon. The ocean roared loudly as it crashed against the cliffs below the golf course.

"You're leaving in a few days. What does it matter what I mean?"

She wrenched her arm from his grasp and surged on, cutting across next door's nature strip to her house.

"Phoebe." He ran to catch up, and this time he didn't think; he reacted purely to the despair on her face. He pulled her close in his arms and kissed her. She resisted, her mouth hard under his. He stopped, released her, stepped back, shaken by her refusal. Was he so repellent to her?

"Sorry." He licked his lips, still tasting her sweetness. "I'm sorry. I shouldn't have done that."

"No." The words hurtled at him from the deep shadows cast by the flowering shrubs along the fence, their perfume cloying in the warm air, sickening and heavy. "No, you shouldn't have."

"Phoebe, I'm sorry. I just couldn't help myself. I wanted to kiss you."

"And then what?" she demanded.

He stepped closer, wary. "We enjoy kissing each other, like we did before . . . I thought. No . . . I didn't think . . ."

"Don't you understand?" She flung her arms wide in exasperation. "What happens is we enjoy kissing each other but . . ." Her voice broke on a half sob; her arms dropped to her sides. "I enjoy it too much and then you go away."

He reached to pull her into his embrace, but she sprang back out of the shadows. "Don't." Were those tears shimmering on her cheeks?

"But, Phoebe . . ."

"But what? You can't deny you're leaving on Friday. You have to. You don't want to stay here."

"I didn't realize kissing you held such implications." He never did with women, until too late.

"Exactly. For you it doesn't. For me . . . I . . ."

Brady stood motionless as her words swirled in his stunned brain. What was she trying to tell him? That she loved him? "What are you saying?" he asked softly. "Phoebe? Are you saying you . . ."

"Love you?" She stared at him. Defiant. Scornful. As if that were the pits.

"Do you?"

"I don't know." Her voice fell and, with it, her gaze. "But I know if I let you touch me or . . . or . . . kiss me, I won't be able to resist you."

"I . . . I had no idea you felt that way about me." He touched a finger to her chin and tilted it up gently. Her eyes were shiny with tears. "I thought you wanted to be friends."

"I do."

"So do I." He swallowed. What she was offering was wonderful, a whole new world of possibility. She was beautiful, perfect, exciting. No other woman came close. Was this love? No sooner had the thought formed than he cast it aside. No. She was an infatuation at best.

"But that's all you want, isn't it? I want more. More than you can give."

How many times had he heard those words from desirable women across the world? If he said what she wanted to hear, he'd be giving up everything he'd dreamed of, everything he'd achieved. He could offer her affection and friendship. He hadn't said it before, and he couldn't say it now, even though Phoebe was the closest thing to perfection he'd seen in his life. He couldn't commit to more, couldn't say he loved her. The thought terrified him. He said what he always said.

"You are the most beautiful girl I've ever met. I was attracted to you the first moment I saw you."

"Stop it! Don't say another word."

She turned and ran for the house. He watched while she let herself in, and then, when a light shone in the living room window, he wandered back the way they'd come, head bowed, feet scuffing softly on the grass verge. It was an infatuation, not love. How could he tell? He'd never had an ache like this before. It was a pain as strong as the toothache, but one that pierced his heart and drained his energy so the effort of lifting one foot after the other was almost beyond him.

But it would pass. Experience told him that. A couple more days and he'd be back to normal. Phoebe would recede into her rightful place in his past, another attractive woman who'd enjoyably filled some otherwise empty days. Another woman who'd professed to love him, and one who made no bones about her desire for marriage and a family.

A closer shave than most but an escape nonetheless.

Phoebe didn't see or hear from Brady until Tuesday, when he appeared for his dental appointment. When it was over, he lingered while she tidied the surgery for the next patient.

"How are you?"

"Fine, thank you." She wiped the basin and replaced the rinse water glass with a clean one.

"Phoebe, would you still like to come to Jeff's for dinner on Thursday? We played golf this morning and he asked. I said I'd check with you."

She'd never seen him so subdued and anxious except when he was about to have the root canal. Was facing her in the knowledge that she might be in love with him akin in his mind to that?

"Would you rather I didn't?"

"No. Why wouldn't I want you to come?"

"You know . . ." His blank expression told her he didn't. "After what I said."

He smiled. "I liked what you said."

"But . . . I was so . . ."

"Honest," he supplied. *Rude* was uppermost in her head, but if he thought *honest,* then fine. But what was he trying to say now?

"Phoebe, you . . ."

Graeme came back in with a folder of X-rays. "Phoebe, would you fetch Mr. Trembath, please?"

"Sorry, I was holding her up," Brady said. He followed her to the waiting room.

"Thursday?"

She nodded. Elderly Mr. Trembath was watching with a twinkle in his eye. He was a regular customer in the bookshop, an avid reader of British whodunits who fancied himself a keen observer of humanity, always on the alert for a clue.

"What time?"

"Seven. They live across the bridge. Can we take Fred?"

"Fine."

"I'll see you then."

"Bye."

The door clicked shut behind him.

"We're ready for you now, Mr. Trembath."

"Good-looking bloke, your young fellow," he said. "New in town, is he?"

"He's not my young fellow." She turned and led him away from Felicity's flapping ears.

"He thinks he is. Take it from an old fellow. I know." He gave a wheezy chuckle.

"He's going back to Europe on Friday. He's a friend, that's all."

"Oh. If you say so." He switched his attention to Graeme. "Ah, here's the torturer himself. Good morning, sir."

Graeme tossed Phoebe a tired little smile. Amazing how many people came in and said things like that to the dentist.

Brady knocked on Phoebe's door at ten to seven on Thursday evening. He smoothed his hair and brushed a wisp of grass from the knee of his jeans, which he'd ironed to go with the one decent shirt he'd brought with him, also newly pressed. It was ridiculous to be nervous. He was like a boy picking up a girl for a first date. Something had changed in their relationship, subtly, when she'd as much as told him she loved him. Somehow that admission had given her the upper hand, and he had no idea why. It was as if he had to prove he was worthy of that love, stop messing about and shape up. Usually it worked the other way round. A woman said she loved him, and his path was clear—to get out before those emotional tentacles took a stranglehold. The feeling he had now was odd and rather unsettling.

When Jeff had repeated his dinner invitation, Brady's first reaction was to say Phoebe couldn't make it. It would save face on both sides. But he didn't; he said he'd check. He wanted her to come. He wanted to show her off to his old friend. He wanted to be with her and make things right between them; this was his only chance before he flew out. If she'd refused, his disappointment would have been unbearable, because he doubted she would allow him to see her alone.

Phoebe had practically admitted she loved him, but she didn't expect anything in return. Was he so much of a write-off as a prospect in her eyes? Depressing thoughts had occupied his mind incessantly, even during the previous day's dive, an activity that normally would have totally absorbed him. He'd spent most of the time wishing Phoebe were there enjoying it with him, but knowing she wouldn't have gone. Did she dive? He didn't know that, along with all the other things he'd never know about her.

The door opened abruptly. She wore a dress he hadn't seen before. It was made of dark red shiny material and had thin straps that went over her smooth tanned shoulders. *Stunning.* She was more beautiful than he remembered, and he'd seen her only two days earlier, on Tuesday.

"Hi." She pulled the door to latch with a solid click. Gold drop earrings swung against her neck.

"You look terrific."

She glanced up with a tiny smile, said, "Thanks," and started down the steps to Fred in the driveway, then looked over her shoulder at him gaping. "Coming?"

"Yes." He spurred himself to action. "Shall I drive?"

She tossed him the keys in answer. "May as well have a farewell spin."

He swallowed and sprinted forward to open her door. If only they were going somewhere alone instead of to Jeff's. He didn't want to share her; he wanted her all to himself that night. He wanted to slide his arm around her waist and hold her close, memorize the feel of her, imprint her on his skin.

"Thanks." Her slim, elegant legs and body folded themselves into the passenger seat with a swish of silky fabric. He closed the door carefully.

Fred was running well now, very smoothly. It was a little thing she might remember him for. He backed down the drive, pausing for a car to pass.

"What's his wife's name again?" she said.

"Gosh!"

"You've forgotten!"

"It'll come to me."

"It'd better." She smirked and looked out her side window. "You're not very good with names, are you?"

"No. You'll have to direct me. Water Crescent," Brady began.

"Are you sure?"

He shot her a quick glance and caught her smile. "Yes. What did you say your name is?"

Laughter gurgled in her throat. "There are some lovely homes there overlooking the inlet. Head across the bridge and turn left immediately."

He dragged his attention from the sound of her laughter to the road. "Jeff's done well for himself."

"Was he a good friend?"

"We caught the same bus to the same school for years, but we didn't hang out together. Not much in common. He was a brainiac, did high-level math and science. Plus he's a year younger than me."

"What did you do at school?"

"Sports, and I liked history, but only the stuff about the sea explorers." Escaping into a world of adventure. Daydreaming of a life unfettered by other people's rules, of being beholden to no one but himself and nature.

"Captain Cook?"

"And all the others. They were amazing sailors."

"Very brave to head off into the unknown and leave their families behind. For years."

Unless you had no family. When he'd left Australia, the vast unknown was the attraction. "Yep. That's what the sea does to you. Once that salt water gets into your blood . . ."

"I'm a landlubber," she admitted.

"You needn't be. I was for the first twenty or so years of my life."

"But you always liked the sea. I like swimming in it, but that's about it."

"Maybe you should give it a try."

"What, sailing? I guess I could ask Phil to take me out. He goes every now and again." She wasn't very keen; in fact, she was uninterested.

He pulled up at a stop sign and waited for a stream of cars. He hadn't meant sailing with Phil. He'd meant . . . what? What was he hinting at? Did he want Phoebe to come with him? She wouldn't. Couldn't. Why wasn't he relieved by the finality of her refusal of his offers, albeit joking, to crew on *Lady Lydia?*

"You might like it." *Leave it. She isn't interested.*

She didn't reply. He nipped across the intersection and turned right. The road swung round the headland and down across the fields, past the campground, to the long, low bridge across the inlet.

"Should we take something for our unnamed hostess? Flowers? Chocolates?" Phoebe asked.

"Good idea. I forgot."

"We can stop at the shops opposite the campground."

When they were under way again, with a bunch of flowers in damp purple paper on the backseat, Phoebe said, "What time's your flight?"

"I'll have to leave Narooma at about twelve-thirty."

"I won't be able to take you to Moruya." She sounded dismayed.

"No, I know. I've booked a taxi." Was she remembering their first day together? The kiss on the beach? He didn't dare ask. She'd made intimate talk off limits.

"So this is the last time we'll see each other," Phoebe said flatly.

"'Fraid so."

He risked a glance to see her expression, but she was looking out the window at the water as they crossed the bridge. *The last time.* It hadn't truly sunk in. He'd never see her again. What did she think of that? She wasn't saying. What did he think of that? Would it be too rude to call Jeff and cry off? Drive on up the coast somewhere and find a secluded place to have dinner, just the two of them? Maybe there would be other guests and they could sneak away early.

"Turn here," she said.

Jeff must have been watching out the window for them, because he flung the door open as they walked up the front steps of the house.

"Hello, Brady." He pumped Brady's hand up and down, then transferred his attention to Phoebe. "You must be Phoebe. I'm so pleased you could come." He gave her hand the same pump-handle treatment, then released her to step back with a sweeping gesture. "Welcome to *chez nous.*"

"Thank you for the invitation," she said.

Brady, clutching the flowers, which were now dripping water from the bottom of the wrapping paper, allowed her to precede him into the house.

"Janette's just putting the finishing touches to the first course," Jeff boomed behind them.

Phoebe turned with a tiny private smile. Her eyes met Brady's for a brief moment, a jewel for him alone, then flashed away to Jeff.

"Janette," she said. "We brought her some flowers."

Brady handed them over with a flourish.

"Lovely. Thank you. She'll love them." Jeff steered the two of them into a wide room with a balcony, which ran almost the length of the house and afforded a breathtaking view over the inlet and, to the left, the bridge and part of the bay.

"Wow!" Brady strode forward to the open sliding door. "Ripper view, mate."

"It's what sold us the house," said Jeff. "What will you have to drink?"

Brady looked at Phoebe. She read his mind.

"I'll drive," she said. "Something soft, thanks, Jeff."

"Beer, thanks."

Jeff headed off with the flowers.

"Janette," Brady murmured.

"Try to remember it." She stepped out onto the balcony and leaned on the railing. He followed.

"That's the house we stayed in." She pointed across to the far side of the inlet. The little jetty he'd walked along was tiny from here, the upper floor of the house just visible through the trees. It seemed a lifetime ago, the wedding party—the one without Phoebe. As would be the rest of his life after tomorrow. He swallowed, surreptitiously edged closer to her so his bare arm brushed hers as they leaned side by side on the railing. She always smelled tantalizingly fresh, like spring flowers.

"It was a good week, wasn't it?" she went on. "Fun. Lindy was lucky to get the house."

"Apart from my tooth it was fun. Good to see Dave and Alex again." If she wasn't mentioning the Lindy drama, he certainly wasn't. He gazed out at the inlet, the light softening now as the sun sank lower. It was still hot, although a light sea breeze danced across the water, bringing the familiar tang of salt and faraway places. "This spot has a better view. You know, your block would have a fantastic view if you had a two-story house on it."

"Mmm. I'd need a fantastic amount of money first."

"Hello, Brady. Hello, Phoebe. Nice to meet you."

Brady straightened and turned, smiling as Jeff and Janette stepped out onto the balcony.

"Janette. Hello."

"Thanks for the lovely flowers."

Jeff handed them each a frosted glass. Ice tinkled in Phoebe's lemon squash.

She said, "We were just admiring your view."

"Yes. We'd been house hunting for a while, but as soon as we saw that, we looked at each other and nodded." Jeff slipped his arm around Janette's waist and squeezed. "We're on the same wavelength."

"Brady said you live in Narooma, Phoebe," said Janette. "What do you do?"

"Yes, I've been here quite a few years now. I worked in Imelda's Preloved Books until last week. Now I'm Graeme Tucker's dental assistant."

"Oh, we know Graeme and Lynn," said Jeff. "Lovely people."

"I haven't met his wife."

Janette said with a knowing smile, "You will. She gives the most fabulous dinner parties. They're such fun. She always has a theme of some sort. She even did one of those murder mystery dinners. Turned out Jeff was the murderer."

Jeff roared with laughter. "We all had to dress up."

"Sounds entertaining," said Brady. It sounded horrible. If there was one thing he hated, it was organized fun. "Sometimes the guests on the yacht have theme parties. We haven't had a murder yet, though."

"We were thinking of having one ourselves." Janette trilled with laughter. "Not a murder, a mystery dinner party. We'll invite you, Phoebe, if we do."

"Thank you."

She looked and sounded sincere. Was his beautiful, vibrant Phoebe really happy to settle into this sort of life? Hanging out with married couples and attending dress-up dinner parties, or visiting retired people, like Ruth and Phil? Having her social life analyzed by well-meaning neighbors?

Phoebe sipped her icy drink. She'd bet her bottom dollar Brady wouldn't dress up if his life depended on it. It wasn't her choice of activity either, but if she was invited by these friendly people, she'd accept. The more people she met, the less time she spent alone, the less she'd be exposed to the gaping hole Brady would leave in her life.

It was their last night together. What a pity they had to spend it here. Not that these two were unpleasant—quite the opposite, they were very nice—but with only hours left before they parted . . . Brady must not care, though, because he'd accepted the invitation for that night, knowing it would be the last time they had together. Her declaration of almost love must have been filed away with all the rest. At least he'd been kind enough not to refer to it.

Stop. Don't get maudlin. He was leaving the next day, and that was that. These were his friends and may well become hers.

"Dinner's ready," said Janette. She led the way through the living room to a dining room, which opened onto another balcony, facing west toward the mountains. A table was set outside with candles glowing in the gathering dusk. "I thought it was such a lovely evening we could eat out here."

Jeff and Brady did most of the talking, fortunately. As the evening progressed, Phoebe had less and less to say. Time was ticking away. Brady sat opposite her, smiling and laughing, reminiscing with Jeff about old school friends and teachers, telling them about his boat and his travels. Jeff roared with laughter at the slightest hint of a joke, and Janette trotted in and out with more and more delicious food, refusing offers of assistance with a smile. Phoebe had no choice but to sit and watch the man she loved slipping away from her with each movement of the hands of the ornate clock facing her through the doorway.

The conversation veered to Asia and the holiday the hosts had taken recently to China.

"I've never been to Asia," said Brady.

"Wonderful place, China. The people are so friendly. We've been to Vietnam too, and Bali."

"I'd like to climb the Great Wall," said Phoebe, so as to seem alert and interested.

"We did that. It was fabulous. So enormous. I've never climbed so many steps in my life as I did in China." Janette placed her hand on Jeff's arm. "We should show them our photos."

"Good idea!" Jeff pushed his chair away. "You finish your coffee and I'll set up the laptop and the TV."

A slide night. Phoebe glanced at Brady. How many photos did they have? A lot, she was sure. Jeff was a very enthusiastic person. He'd photograph everything, every step on the Great Wall, every brick in the imperial palace. It was almost nine-thirty. They wouldn't be able to leave until at least eleven, probably. She had an early start in the morning. Someone was coming in for an appointment at seven-thirty.

Janette said, "Would you like to see them?" Her eager expression indicated very clearly what their response should be.

"I would," said Brady. Phoebe nodded. Maybe she'd get to sit close to him on the couch.

"Bring your cups in with you and I'll make fresh coffee." Janette sprang to her feet, plunger pot in hand. "We'll be in the living room. If you need to freshen up, the bathroom is down the hall and second on the left." She disappeared in a flurry of floral-print skirt.

Phoebe pushed her chair back and stood up. Brady said, "Do you mind?"

"Do you?"

"We needn't stay too long."

"I have an early start tomorrow, that's all. Seven-thirty."

"Cripes." He grimaced. "Okay, we'll try to leave by ten-thirty."

"Fine." An hour or two at the most left with him. She stepped into the dining room. "I've always wanted to climb the Great Wall of China."

He stopped. "Have you?"

She stopped and turned, close to him, looking up into his face. "Yes. Why are you so surprised?"

"I thought you were happy staying here, that you didn't want to go anywhere else."

What if she kissed him, just a little kiss on the cheek? Her fingers curled against her palm in the effort to resist. The other hand gripped the empty coffee cup.

"I don't want to *live* on the Great Wall of China. I'd have a look and then come back. I never said I didn't want to travel and see other places." She shrugged. "But I don't have the luxury of traveling anywhere at the moment." She turned away, hollow inside despite the food she'd eaten.

His hand landed lightly on her arm, fingers warm. Her breath jammed. "Phoebe, you could . . . I . . ."

"All set," called Ringmaster Jeff from the living room. "Hurry, hurry. Show's about to start."

Brady's eyes locked with hers for a moment. Were they trying to tell her something? What? She waited, breath stuck, an indigestible lump in her throat. A tiny frown hovered on his brow. He looked away.

"Come on," he murmured.

She trailed after him but changed her mind and found the bathroom first. If they were in for an extended showing, she needed to be prepared. What had he been about to say? That she could come and crew on his boat? She couldn't. Wouldn't. Unless he offered more. He wouldn't.

Brady sat on one end of the big white leather sofa facing the large flat television screen mounted on the wall. Jeff's laptop was on the coffee table along with fresh coffee and almond biscuits. Set for the night—a long night.

"Help yourself." Janette smiled when Phoebe reappeared. "You sit there next to Brady."

"Thanks. I couldn't eat another thing. In fact, I won't need to eat for days." She sank into the soft leather. He was inches away. His body radiated warmth.

Brady laughed. "Me neither. It was a terrific dinner, Janette. Thank you very much."

"She's a great cook." Jeff clicked off the overhead light, leaving only the gentle glow from a standing lamp in the corner. "Now, here we go. This is us at Sydney airport checking in." Two almost identical photos flashed onto the screen a couple of seconds apart. The first showed a grinning Janette with two red suitcases by her legs, and the second, a grinning Jeff with the two red suitcases by his legs. The next was of the interior of the plane; the next taken out the window at altitude. Clouds. And more clouds. The next was of the in-flight dinner they were served.

Brady sighed softly. Phoebe nudged his side with her elbow under cover of the dim lighting. He moved his leg so his thigh touched hers lightly. By accident?

"I hate flying," he said.

"I love it," cried Janette. "It's so exciting going somewhere new."

"That's true. I like that aspect. It's the physical bit I hate. All crammed in together with that horrible recycled air and the nonstop roar of those engines."

"I've never been on a plane," said Phoebe. Her whole leg tingled in response to Brady's touch. "I don't have a passport."

"Haven't you?" Jeff and Janette chorused. The next photos flashed up. A large crowded airport.

"Shanghai. It's got the most extraordinary design," said Jeff. Then came shots of enormous buildings, traffic, people, bicycles, and a wide river with ships and all sorts of smaller boats.

Brady said, "I'd love to sail up there."

"Piracy can be a problem in some of those waters," said Jeff.

Phoebe shuddered. Yachtsmen were killed and their boats ransacked and stolen. Even big ships were attacked. Brady wouldn't be so reckless. . . .

"I've often thought of sailing around the world."

"Gosh! What a wonderful idea." Janette almost squealed with delight. "Don't you think, Phoebe? Just imagine sailing into those exotic harbors. Tahiti, Jamaica, Acapulco, Rio."

"Narooma," Jeff said, and cackled. "Could you get your boat in through the breakwater, do you think, Brady?"

"Doubt it. I wouldn't like to try. She's a bit big and far too valuable to risk crashing on those rocks at the entrance. I don't want *Lady Lydia* to become a dive attraction like the *Lady Darling.*"

"This is us on the river cruise at night. That's the Bund." Another photo appeared on-screen. It was very dark with splotches of bright color here and there and the vague outlines of buildings.

"The night lights are amazing in Shanghai. All different colors and patterns. You can't see it very well from photos." More of the same flashed on the screen; then suddenly there was a beautifully clear shot of an ancient Chinese multistory wooden building with a zigzag bridge over an ornamental pond.

"How lovely," Phoebe said.

"It is. They made the bridge that way so attacking soldiers were slowed down by the angles and couldn't storm across," said Jeff. "Very clever people, the Chinese. They invented all sorts of things way before we in the West were even functioning properly as societies."

"Fascinating," said Phoebe. It was too—just not right now, when all she wanted was to be with Brady. Alone. He hadn't moved his leg.

The trek across China culminated ninety minutes later in Beijing, the Rogerses having viewed the Terracotta Warriors in Xi'an, scaled a steep rocky mountain called Hua Shan to visit yet another temple, and climbed up and down the Great Wall from as many angles as Jeff could manage.

Janette switched the light on. Jeff turned off his electronic gadgets. "How about a nightcap?" he said. "I have a very nice cognac we brought back duty-free."

Brady stood up. "No, thanks, Jeff. We really should go. It's getting late." Phoebe rose as well and took a couple of hopeful steps toward the door.

"No, no, it's early. Not midnight yet." Jeff flung his arms wide. "The night is yet young."

"Thank you for the photos. It's made me keen to go to China," said Phoebe to Janette, who'd begun to collect the empty coffee cups and put them on a tray. "Maybe I should apply for a passport just in case I get the chance to travel one day."

"Good idea," said Brady. "Be ready."

"You should." Janette's eyes lit up. "I bought the most beautiful silks at the markets so cheaply. Fabulous rolls of dress fabric, scarves, and even a silk quilt and cover from that silk factory we showed you in Shanghai. Come and see. It won't take a minute."

She abandoned her clearing up and headed for a door at the far end of the room.

Phoebe glanced helplessly at Brady, but Jeff already had him by the arm. "While they're doing that, Brady, I'd like your opinion. I'm thinking of buying a little runabout—a boat. For fishing and taking people out, et cetera. I have the brochures and info in my study."

Brady tried again. "We really mustn't stay too long."

"I have an early start in the morning," said Phoebe.

"Just a couple of minutes." Jeff was already beetling out another door and down the hallway.

Twenty minutes later, Phoebe made her last exclamation over what really were the most beautiful colors and cloths she'd ever seen, all strewn in an exotic muddle on the spare bed, and said firmly, "We'll have to go, Janette. I'm sorry." The little bedside clock had just displayed 11:56 in bright green. "I have to be at work at seven."

"Yes. We have to be up early too, but we're having so much fun it's hard to say good night, isn't it?"

Apparently it was. Phoebe smiled. "Yes. It's been a lovely evening. Thank you."

"We must keep in touch now we've met."

"I'd like that." She ran her fingers lightly over a fringed scarf of deep red silk shot with gold thread. "And I would love to go to China one day."

"Get that passport as a first step, keep thinking positive, and it'll happen one day. Wouldn't it be fun to go cruising round the Med on Brady's boat?" Janette picked up the scarf and folded it. "Take this, Phoebe. As a gift and to remind you to go to China."

"No, I couldn't." Janette made travel sound so easy. Was it? Was thinking positive going to make Brady love her the way she loved him?

"Why not? Look how many I have, and I've already given lots away as gifts. I just went shopping mad in the markets, couldn't resist. I'm a good bargainer, so they were very cheap. Please take it."

"If you're sure . . . Thank you. I'd love to." The rich fabric lay in a smooth, soft bundle in her hands. It was gorgeous and exotic.

"Oh good." Janette actually clapped with delight. "Red suits you."

Brady and Jeff were still in his study, bent over the desk, discussing boats.

"Phoebe wants to leave now," Janette said.

Brady straightened swiftly. "Oh, sorry. We got absorbed here."

"Look what Janette gave me." Phoebe held out the scarf.

"It's beautiful. Red suits you." His eyes embraced her.

"Silk is surprisingly warm," said Jeff. "And incredibly strong but very light and fine. They said you should be able to pull good-quality silk fabric through your wedding ring."

"Goodness." If she had one, she'd try.

"Amazing," Brady said. "Well, thanks for a lovely evening and terrific dinner, Janette."

"It was an absolute pleasure. I was just saying to Phoebe how much fun it's been."

"Next time you come to town, you must let us know," said Jeff.

"You won't be back, will you?" Phoebe looked Brady directly in the eye, but before he could reply, Janette said, "We'll have to come and visit you and hire your boat, won't we, Phoebe?"

"Ooh! A cruise round Italy and the French Riviera sounds just the ticket. We were thinking of doing Europe next time." Jeff flung his arm around Janette's shoulders. "We're intrepid adventurers."

"Not quite as intrepid as Brady, though," said Janette, "from what you told us over dinner—packing up and leaving home for good when you finished university with no plans and nowhere to go."

"Alex and Dave came too," he said.

"But they came home after six months. You didn't. That was very brave, going it alone like that," Janette insisted.

"I didn't have a home to leave. Not really. When I went to university, I left the foster home I was living in when I knew Jeff. I didn't think it was brave. To me it was an escape. It was exciting. I like being alone, making my own decisions."

"I make my own decisions," said Jeff. "So does Janette, but we discuss them with each other, and we think the same way and want the same things from life, so generally we support each other very well. And it's more fun with two. The good things. I certainly don't feel stifled. Do you?" He turned to Janette.

She shook her head. "We're very happy. But we're lucky, because we found each other. Some people probably don't find each other, which is sad."

Brady said nothing. He stuck out his hand. "Good-bye, Jeff. I'm glad you said hello that day."

"Me too. Good luck."

Kisses and hugs flew, good-byes were called to float on the cool night air, and finally Phoebe pulled Fred's door closed and started the engine.

Brady heaved a vast sigh beside her. Phoebe yawned.

"Tired?"

"I wasn't, but now I am suddenly."

She swung Fred onto the bridge. Moonlight glittered in a silver path across the bay, but clouds had gathered on the horizon, a thick, dark band building to envelop the moon.

"That was very nice of Janette to give me a scarf." Not what she wanted to say at all.

"Yes. They're both nice people. Very generous."

What she wanted to say was too big and too complex, and she didn't really understand it herself. Or maybe it was just too simple to blurt out. Three simple words: *I love you.* She'd hinted it before, almost said it, but failed at the last. She wasn't brave enough. It was too late now. Nothing would be achieved; nothing would change, except she'd possibly be humiliated by his compassionate acceptance of her declaration. Because he was a kind man and wouldn't deliberately embarrass or hurt her.

He'd kiss her with great gentleness and hold her in his arms. And say good-bye. With relief.

Chapter Twelve

As they reached the brow of the hill near the golf course, almost home, Brady said, "Want to know what I said to Sophie?"

"When?" That had come out of the blue. Sophie hadn't entered her head since the wedding.

"In Italian. Remember that day at lunch?" When he'd fixed Sophie with a seductive gaze and lowered his voice to an intimate level.

"Oh yes. Sophie was very impressed." When Phoebe had been annoyed and envious of the way the two girls claimed his attention, even though she knew his kisses had been given to her with the same degree of attraction he showed to them: superficial. "I'd forgotten."

"I said, *'Non mi sente bene perche ho mal di dente,'* which means 'I'm not feeling very well, because I have a toothache.'"

Phoebe giggled, partly from relief, partly from amusement. "I'm sure she thought it was something much more seductive." And he'd intended her to. He'd been flirting. He couldn't help himself.

"What did you think I said?"

"I didn't know."

"I wasn't interested in Sophie or Kate."

What was he expecting her to say to that? She said nothing. She turned into her driveway and stopped. The silence was vast after Fred's roar.

"Just so you know."

Why say that? Why? Was he trying to make her feel better about loving him by assuring her he wasn't attracted to anyone else either? Phoebe turned to him, fingers on the door handle. "It's too late, Brady." She flung the door open and got out. His door slammed; feet crunched on gravel.

He stood in front of her, blocking the path to the house.

"Too late for what?"

"Anything. Everything." She exhaled. All the longing, all the frustration, all the love she had for him poured into the night air and disappeared into the dark. With it went her energy and any vestiges of hope that he might suddenly change, have a complete reversal of attitude, reexamine a view of life forged in a sad childhood by a broken family and a series of less-than-happy substitutes. A couple of weeks in her company wouldn't achieve the impossible no matter how much she wished. "I'm tired."

He extended his arms and drew her, unresisting, against his chest. She leaned against his shirt, a button pressed into her cheek, his chin rested on her head.

"I'll miss you," he murmured.

A tear ran slowly down her face and hovered near her top lip. She licked it away. Salty. Her arms tightened around his waist. If she held on tight enough, would he stay? If she closed her eyes, would time stop?

"I can't stay," he said.

"I know."

"But I would if I could."

Stupid, stupid dreaming. Childish. Grow up, Phoebe.

"Sure." She released her grip and pushed him away. "Go."

"Phoebe . . ."

"Good night. Good-bye."

"I wish I could say what you want me to, but . . ."

"Just go, Brady. Safe travels."

She hesitated a split second, staring up into his face, memorizing his eyes, the lock of hair that fell across his brow, the angle of his nose, his mouth—then spun about, fumbling for her keys as she ran toward the steps.

"Good-bye." He made no move to catch her; he just waited while she opened the door, standing motionless and silent beside the dark bulk of Fred in the driveway.

He was gone. No early-morning call before she left for work, no midmorning call before he left for Moruya. Her summer love was over. Her unrequited summer love, which had turned into a unique summer torture. At least she had a job she enjoyed and two new friends, but they wouldn't make up for what was missing, what had always been missing but had never been apparent before.

It wasn't the wedding or the prospect of a family; it was the love. A depth of love she had never before experienced and she now recognized as the driving force behind the countless marriages she'd performed. Loving someone and knowing they loved you. What a priceless gift. What a rare treasure, one now lost to her because the man she loved didn't feel the same way and she couldn't imagine loving anyone else the way she loved Brady Winters.

The days following his departure became a blur, merging one into the other. She dreaded the weekend, but surprisingly, she slept deep, dreamless sleeps and woke late on both Saturday and Sunday, when she'd expected to toss and turn all night. Maybe it was the cooler temperatures heralded by the massed clouds on Thursday night; maybe it was the letdown after three or more weeks of unusual emotional activity; but her body sank into a state of torpor from which she roused herself by sheer willpower.

She called in to the pharmacy late Saturday morning to thank Jeff for dinner, and she called Gavin and spent a drizzling, damp Sunday afternoon catching up on Imelda's doings. His grumbling reports of Imelda's latest irrationalities made her glad not to be involved, and irritated by Gavin's unquestioning acceptance of such behavior. Then it was Monday, and more teeth.

On Wednesday a postcard arrived in the mail along with Fred's registration renewal and a council notice about water conservation. The postcard had a picture of the Sydney Harbour Bridge. Phoebe studied it for a few moments, wondering who she knew in Sydney, then turned it over. Unfamiliar writing. Half printing, half cursive. Written by someone who didn't write by hand very much.

Dear Phoebe,

   I'm sorry we parted the way we did. I wanted to say thank you for taking care of me these last weeks. I would never have survived without you.

                                                                Brady Winters

Brady Winters. Full name, as if he feared she'd forgotten him already. He would have survived without her. That was his specialty: survival. He certainly didn't need a woman to care for him.

But he must have bought the card at the airport before he left the country, gone to the trouble of finding a stamp and a postbox, thinking of her.

She stuck the postcard on the fridge next to the one John and Margaret had sent from Paris. Maybe she should apply for a passport, a small gesture toward breaking out. Her pay was better now; she could maybe afford a holiday one day. But then her stomach sagged and a rush of tears threatened to choke her. *Alone.* She'd be alone. Unlike Brady, she wasn't brave. And she wanted to share the fun of travel with someone. *Brady.* Only with Brady. The way Jeff and Janette did.

Ten days later a letter arrived. A handwritten letter with Greek stamps. She recognized the writing immediately. Her fingers trembled as she tore the envelope open.

Dear Phoebe,

I'm no good at writing letters. I can't remember when I last wrote to someone—but then, I don't have anyone to write to. Except you. I want to write to you, which is strange. I don't mean strange that anyone would want to write to you. I mean strange that I have this compulsion. I'd rather talk to you— hear your voice. But I'm worse at saying some things. I'm not very good at any of it.

There was a gap here, as if he'd stopped and then begun again later. The writing was smaller, more compact and controlled, the lines straighter.

It's three o'clock in the morning now, and I'm sitting on the plane, surrounded by people trying to sleep. I think we're somewhere over the Indian Ocean. The woman next to me gave me this paper and the pen. I didn't have anything to write with. I started to write but didn't know what to say, so I'm trying again.

Some loser nicked my phone going through security at Sydney, so I've lost all my contacts. I never had your number anyway, and I don't have your e-mail address, so I can't contact you any other way. I didn't need them before because we were in the same house and I saw you every day. Please e-mail me. bwinters@ladylydia.com

I hope you're enjoying the job at the dentist. I'm so sorry about that first day. You must have hated me and with good cause. But it did work out all right in the end, so I hope I'm forgiven.

The second page was on hotel stationery. Hotel Acropolis, Athens.

I'm in Athens finally. It was one hell of a trip, but at least I didn't have a toothache this time! No more flying for me if I can possibly avoid it. But you might enjoy it. Jeff and Janette do. Have you applied for your passport yet?

I'm joining Lady Lydia tomorrow. Looking forward to it. The weather's cold and wet.

Brady

PS E-mail me. Please.

Phoebe read it through three times before taking it to her bedroom to read again, sitting on her bed. What did it mean? He was missing her? He wanted a pen pal? What would she say if she e-mailed? This letter was written in transit, halfway between here and there, stranded in time, when he was tired and stressed by flying and losing his phone.

She opened her laptop and typed his address into an e-mail. How to start?

Dear Brady,

Thank you for the postcard. It's on the fridge next to one from John and Margaret when they went to Paris. I love postcards.

The job is fine. Don't worry about getting me fired. I saw Gavin a while back, and Imelda is crazier than ever, so I'm glad I'm out of there. I don't know why he stays, but I suppose if you hadn't come along, I'd still be there too. I'm not very brave when it comes to making major changes like that. Not like you.

It's much cooler now and we've had some rain.

She stopped typing. How to sign off? Cheers? She used that with friends. Brady was a friend. She wanted to say *Love* but couldn't. She typed

Best wishes,

Phoebe

And clicked SEND before she could rethink.

He didn't reply for a week. She checked her e-mail at every opportunity and double-checked her sent message to ensure the address was correct—too many times for sanity. It didn't bounce, so it must have arrived. Or whirled into cyberspace oblivion. Should she e-mail again? Would that be desperate?

Another postcard arrived, sent a day after the letter. It was a company postcard of the *Lady Lydia* in full sail on a sparkling blue sea. No wonder he loved it. Sleek and white, cutting through the waves as though the boat loved every minute of it. On the back he wrote,

Dear Phoebe,
  Isn't she beautiful?

Brady

Sometime during the week, Lindy sent photos from the wedding, and Phoebe gazed at Brady's face, trying to remember his voice and his touch, his smell. Everyone looked happy and carefree when it was so nearly a disaster of her own making. It all seemed long ago, distant, a dream. He'd stood by her when it came to the crunch, even though he'd thought she was wrong. "We'll face the music together," he'd said when they returned from Phil and Ruth's that horrible night and she was reluctant to enter the house. She closed her eyes and imagined his embrace, remembered his kiss on her lips. But when she opened them, she was still alone with an aching empty heart.

She stared at the postcard of the *Lady Lydia,* trying to imagine him on deck, raising and lowering the sails, giving orders to his crew, enjoying the freedom. Happy and fulfilled, the way he'd looked on their relatively tame excursion to Montague Island.

Then, finally, a message arrived.

Dear Phoebe,

Thank you for replying. I wasn't sure you would. We've had some dramas here with the boat, which I won't bore you with, but all's well now. I'm so sorry I didn't reply sooner. You must have thought I didn't care, when I do.

Brady

He'd been busy. Still was, judging by the curtness of the message. Of course. She wasn't a priority. He had clients and a crew to manage, plus his boat. The all-consuming *Lady Lydia*. His love.

She didn't reply. Not immediately. Maybe she would the next day or even the day after, when she'd had time to think. Now she had to leave or be late for work.

Two days later she wrote,

Dear Brady,

I hope the Lady Lydia is all fixed. Thank you for the post-card. She really is beautiful, and I can see why you love her.

We had our own little drama here. Remember John from next door? He fell off a chair last night changing a lightbulb and broke his arm. Margaret came running over in a panic. Luckily I was home and could drive them to hospital. He's all right, but Margaret has forbidden him to do anything round the house. He can't anyway with a pink cast on his arm!

Janette rang me at work today with an invitation to one of their murder mystery nights. I'm not sure I want to go, but I probably will. I know you wouldn't. I'd have to dress up as a famous opera singer. I hope I don't have to sing. What did your Dutch lady wear?

Again the doubt about the sign-off. He hadn't put anything, just his name. So she did the same.

Phoebe

Bland and boring, but this was her life. For a few sparkling weeks, the humdrum became fun; her little house came alive; her world expanded beyond the confines of this small community. Brady would soon tire of her parochial snippets of news, and his e-mails would trickle to a halt. He might send the occasional postcard. At the moment he was clinging to the memory of an odd summer break, nothing more.

His reply came overnight. She read it while she had a late breakfast on Saturday before heading out to do a lunchtime wedding in Bermagui and then back home for a five o'clock service up the road at the golf club. It was a busy day.

Dear Phoebe,

Sorry to hear about John. He was lucky not to have had worse injuries. I bet he loves that pink cast. I can picture it. Hahaha. It was nice that Jeff and Janette invited you. I know they liked you a lot. You're right. I'd HATE an evening like that. But I also don't enjoy the thought of you going alone to those things. I think if I were still in Narooma and you really wanted to go, I might go with you and that would make it bearable. Being with you makes a lot of unpleasant things bearable—like root canals. ☺

Sorry, have to go. My watch.

B

Phoebe smiled as she read "like root canals." He could have added weddings; he probably thought it. The smile drooped. If he were still in Narooma, they'd do lots of things together, and it would be so much more fun. But he wasn't, and there was no point wishing he was.

That evening she typed,

Dear Brady,

I did two weddings today. They were both lovely and the weather was perfect. You don't need to worry about me going about on my own. Like you, I've done it most of my life and I'm used to it. I chose this life the way you chose yours. I like being settled in one place, whereas I know you don't. You might have enjoyed staying here for a few weeks, but I doubt you'd like it

as a permanent thing. When I travel, which I really would like to do one day, I'll always come home to my blue house.
I did enjoy having you here, though.

Phoebe

Then, when she dragged herself out of bed on Sunday morning, another message waited.

Dear Phoebe,

I might enjoy living ashore, given the right circumstances. Sitting on your deck in the evening with the view of the mountains was great. With you there, of course. It was comfortable and easy. We really did get on very well together. I miss that.

I miss our chats about nothing much and the way you laugh at weird things. I love it when you laugh. You have the most beautiful smile. I hated myself for taking that lovely smile from your face when I first arrived, and for some time after. Some days I'd been so stupid and insensitive I wondered if you'd ever smile at me again.

I wish you could see the view I have right at the moment. There's a perfect rainbow arching across the whole sky. Off to the west it's raining and the sky is thick with dark clouds, but here it's clear and sunny.

I miss you, sweet Phoebe. And I hate the thought of you being in your blue house all alone.

Brady

What was he saying? Phoebe stared at the screen. *'Sweet Phoebe'? He missed her?* Was he just saying that in a fit of nostalgia? All those things, those reminiscences, were they the result of Brady's drinking some powerful Greek brew, staring at a beautiful view, and becoming mellow and a little homesick for a home he'd experienced for three short, unusual weeks? A girl he kissed a couple of times?

Her mouth tightened against a rush of tears. She couldn't bear it if that were the case. How could she possibly tell? Did he realize how he was torturing her? It was easy to type those words from a safe distance, half a world away. She mustn't encourage him. She'd wait at least a week before she replied, and if he persisted, she'd have to put an end to it. A clean break. He could e-mail Alex or Dave and reminisce. She closed the message with a decisive click and went to work.

He e-mailed again. The message was there when she checked after dinner for a message from a prospective bridal couple. It had been sent a few hours after the first.

Darling Phoebe,

I really miss you. Desperately. I knew I would. I told you that last horrible night when it was about all I could say. I wanted to tell you so much more but didn't know how to start. Leaving you was the hardest thing I've ever done in my life. You said I was braver than you because I left Australia and made major changes. I don't think that was brave. I don't think I'm brave. I was running away back then, and I didn't have the guts to tell you how I feel about you a couple of weeks ago. I ran away to sea again.

I'm sitting here staring at the screen and wishing you were here. Lindy e-mailed me some photos from the wedding, so at least I can see your beautiful face whenever I want. But it's not enough. I want you here with me. I want to touch you and hold you in my arms and kiss you. I want to see your smile and hear your laugh, your beautiful joyous laugh.

Jeff said something that stuck in my head. He basically said, 'Sharing the good things is more fun.' I think he's right. I didn't before. Before I met you. We had such a good time together. I loved being with you even when we weren't doing anything special—eating dinner together, at the supermarket, or driving to and from your work. It felt right, and I understand now what you mean when you say you want a family. Two people are the beginning of a family.

But I want to share the wonderful things I see every day. The Greek Islands rising from the sea with their ancient rocky cliffs and white sandy beaches. Fishing villages where we anchor in the harbor and go ashore to eat at a taverna. Sunsets. Lady Lydia *crashing through the waves in full sail. Dawn breaking over the ocean. The nights at sea with more stars in the inky sky than you ever imagined existed. I want you to en-joy it too. I know you'd love it.*

You almost said you loved me once, Phoebe. That was brave. I was staggered. I never dared hope you were feeling what I was trying so hard to deny to myself. You always seemed anxious to be rid of me. I can understand why you pushed me away. You knew more about me than I did. You knew I was incapable of saying what you were able to say. You knew I would have to realize it myself or there was no point. If you felt about me the way I feel about you, I must have broken your heart with my silence. I hope I haven't lost you with my stupid-ity and my fear. I can say it now. I've realized the truth, be-cause I've been confronted with the unbearable alternative. Life without you.

I love you.
Brady

Tears streamed down her cheeks. She didn't bother wiping them, couldn't move, anyway. His words transfixed her. She reached the end and released a pent-up burst of air held unwittingly as she read. Then her hands covered her face, and the tears dripped between her fingers and ran down her chin and onto her throat. She sniffed and laughed and groped for a tissue, didn't find one, so she used the hem of her T-shirt instead.

I love you, he'd said. *I love you.*

"I love you, Brady Winters," she cried aloud. "I love you I love you I love you."

She hit REPLY, typed,

I love you.
Phoebe

and hit SEND.

But what would happen now? He was there and she was here. It was very easy to shout *I love you* across the world, safely from the far side. He wasn't saying *I'll sell up and live with you in Narooma* or even *I'll sail* Lady Lydia *to Narooma to be with you.* He wasn't asking her to join him. He knew what she wanted; she'd made that clear. Was this love without a future?

Nevertheless she went to bed on a wave of euphoria. Brady had said amazing things, things she was positive he'd never said to anyone before. He hadn't even allowed himself to admit the possibility of sharing his life with a woman. He'd been adamant about it. Even his two best friends couldn't convince him to soften his opinion. The very strength of his previous opposition gave credence to the idea that he really meant what he'd written to her. He didn't speak lightly of love. When he spoke, or wrote, those words, she believed him.

Phoebe woke early and opened her laptop eagerly for his response. Nothing. She checked her e-mail first thing in the morning and first thing on returning home in the evening. Nothing. This waiting was almost worse than thinking he didn't care.

He didn't reply. She told herself over and over he was at sea. Captain Brady had responsibilities, just as she did. Things happened at sea. Boats were fragile, and the elements unpredictable. Storms happened at sea. Communications broke down. Then, after two days of silence, she started worrying. She had silly, baseless worries with no understanding of what was really involved in his charter business and the conditions, or even knowledge of where he actually was.

The world weather reports on the multicultural TV channel gave no indication of unusually violent weather patterns. There were no cyclones, volcanic eruptions, or tidal waves. The news gave no reports of pirate attacks or sinkings, boat collisions or drownings in the Aegean and surrounds.

Nothing. Had he lost his nerve again when she replied, declaring her own love so plainly? Had she scared him off?

A postcard arrived with a picture of a bumpy line of orange-roofed white buildings sparkling in the bright sun, facing a harbor full of fishing boats. It was posted on a Greek island called Aegina two days after his letter.

Hi, Phoebe.

*   It's raining. Not like the picture. Wish I was back in Narooma in the heat.*

*   Brady*

She stuck it next to the Harbour Bridge, Paris, and *Lady Lydia*. His reply sat in her in-box on the third day.

Your reply made me laugh with happiness. You say so easily what I took pages to say in my stumbling, inarticulate way. I want to kiss you. It's so frustrating being on opposite sides of the world.

I love you more than anything. For the first time, I wish I was somewhere other than on board Lady Lydia. *We have another week with these clients; then it's back to Piraeus for the next lot and a trip to Crete the following week. I may not be able to e-mail very often, but don't worry. I'll be thinking of you.*

All my love,
Brady

Phoebe replied.

Dearest Brady,

I wish I was with you too. We wasted so much time before you left. I wish I'd said straight-out that I loved you that night after dinner with Ruth and Phil. You would have known then, and maybe you would have said the same to me. I didn't because I was so sure you weren't very interested in me, and I couldn't bear to hear you gently turn me down. My heart nearly did break when you left, but because you'd never given me any indication of your feelings, I figured it was my problem. I had to get over it. It may have taken me years or a lifetime, if ever, I think.

I want to kiss you. I want you to kiss me. I can hardly stand it now that I know how you feel. If I had enough money, I'd fly to Greece tomorrow. But I don't. (Plus I don't have a passport!)

All my love,
Phoebe

This time when he didn't respond immediately, she didn't worry. Another postcard arrived, with a picture of a heavily laden donkey standing on a path with whitewashed houses on either side. This was sent a week after the *Lady Lydia* card.

Dear Phoebe,

I'm not sure any of these postcards will reach you—or when. Mail can be erratic, to say the least. Hope you're well.

Brady

Ten days later a bouquet arrived at the surgery. Felicity called her to the reception desk. They were red roses. Masses of them.

"Lucky you!" Felicity whispered as the phone rang. She turned away to answer it.

Brady. They must be from him. He knew she wouldn't be at home to receive them. Now that he'd succumbed to his feelings at last, he'd become very romantic in his e-mails, as though a logjam had finally broken and he was free to express previously dammed-up emotions. She carried the bouquet into the staff room, away from the curious gazes of Felicity and Mrs. Gibb, from the news agency, who was the biggest gossip in town.

She unwrapped the flowers and stuck them into a plastic container filled with water. A little card was attached. *Love from Brady xxxxx*

Long-distance love was tough. How long would it last fueled only by memories and dreaming? Phoebe touched the ruby-red petals with a gentle finger. Longer than these flowers? Hers would. His was new and novel to him, something strange and exciting, for the moment. Doubts might creep in the longer they were apart. The girl in Narooma might become a nostalgic memory. A summer madness. A "thank goodness she's on the far side of the world."

Graeme stuck his head in. "Ready for Mrs. Gibb?"

"Sorry." At this rate she'd be fired and never be able to save enough money to travel anywhere. She threw a final glance at the roses. Deep, rich red. The symbol of everlasting true love.

Brady loved her.

Two days later, shortly after she arrived at work in the morning, Felicity called her to the desk again. The postman stood there with a letter and a clipboard.

"Sign here, please."

Phoebe scrawled her signature on the form and took the envelope he handed her. "Thanks."

"Are you using the surgery as a dummy address? First flowers, then registered letters. Anyone would think there was something going on." Felicity gave her a narrow-eyed accusing look, then burst out laughing. "It's that gorgeous guy, isn't it? The root canal from the wedding. Brady Winters."

Phoebe nodded, grinning. Fortunately no patients had arrived yet to witness her stoplight impersonation.

"He must be besotted, sending you roses all the way from Europe. I wish I had a guy fall for me like that." She pointed to the letter. "What's that? Is it from him?"

"I've no idea." The envelope was thick and covered with stamps and registered mail stickers. The postmark was illegible apart from the word *Hellas.* Greece.

"Don't stare at it, open it. Here, use this." Felicity handed over a letter opener.

Phoebe slit the top and pulled out several sheets of paper. One was a colored paper cover with a name in Greek and another sheet folded inside. It was typed in English: *Travel Itinerary.*

Her heart bounced in her chest, her legs failed her, and she sat down abruptly on one of the chairs for clients.

Her name was there: *Phoebe Curtis, passenger.* Flying from Sydney to Paris. A flight number and a date. May 26. Two months away. Three days before her birthday. She read down the page. Return booking: Paris to Sydney, November 20.

She swallowed and opened the letter with trembling, clumsy fingers.

Dearest Phoebe,

I know you like surprises, so here is a big one. We can celebrate your birthday in Paris (Lindy told me the date). Please let me do this. I know you'll protest that you can't take such a gift, but I'm being selfish. I want you with me. If you don't use the ticket, then that's your choice. It won't change how I feel about you. Nothing will alter that. If you do use it and for some reason, any reason, you want to go home, you can use the return anytime you want. The date is flexible and can be changed.

I hope you don't, or at least if you do, I'll be returning with you. I know you want security and you love your blue house, but that will always be there, and the thing about living on a boat is that home is mobile. Lady Lydia *can sail in Australian waters just as well as here. Imagine sailing her to Australia together! We can go anywhere we want. Charters off the Queensland coast would be just as viable as here.*

If you make the trip, I promise I won't let you down. I'll be waiting with arms open wide to hold you and protect you for the rest of our lives. I will be your security, and you will be mine.

Phoebe, we've both talked about being brave or not brave. Let's be brave together. Let's jump into the unknown holding hands.

Please say yes.

Your Brady

Five minutes later Phoebe told a disappointed Graeme Tucker she would be leaving in two months. At lunchtime she nipped across to the post office for a passport application, and that evening she e-mailed Brady.

Darling Brady,
Your surprise arrived today.
Yes Yes Yes

Your Phoebe

F Rose
Rose, Elisabeth, 1951-

The wedding party